MILL

Centenary Collection

**Celebrating 100 years of romance with
the very best of Mills & Boon**

*First published in Great Britain 2008
by Harlequin Mills & Boon Limited,
Eton House, 18-24 Paradise Road, Richmond, Surrey TW9 1SR*

© Carole Mortimer 2002

ISBN: 978 0 263 86623 0

77-1208

*Harlequin Mills & Boon policy is to use papers that are
natural, renewable and recyclable products and made from
wood grown in sustainable forests. The logging and
manufacturing processes conform to the legal environmental
regulations of the country of origin.*

*Printed and bound in Spain
by Litografia Rosés S.A., Barcelona*

A Heavenly Christmas

by
Carole Mortimer

MILLS & BOON®
Pure reading pleasure

Carole Mortimer was born in England, the youngest of three children. She began writing in 1978 and has now written over one hundred and forty books for Mills & Boon. Carole has four sons, Matthew, Joshua, Timothy and Peter, and a bearded collie called Merlyn. She says, 'I'm happily married to Peter senior; we're best friends as well as lovers, which is probably the best recipe for a successful relationship. We live in a lovely part of England.'

CHAPTER ONE

'YOU wanted me?'

Mrs Heavenly was aware of the soft, fluttering sensation behind her that told her she was no longer alone. But her attention was so intent upon the vision that she didn't want to leave it, even for a second!

At last! She had waited a long time for this particular plea for help to come. Almost too long, she acknowledged ruefully. But at last it *had* come.

She looked up to smile warmly at the young angel who stood before her. Faith. Yes, she would be perfect for this particular assignment. Warm, compassionate, and with a mischievous sense of humour that had almost been her undoing a couple of times in the past. But in this particular case Faith's qualities were more suited to the problem than the equally admirable ones of Hope or Charity.

'Come and look at this, my dear.' Mrs Heavenly encouraged the angel to step forward and share the vision with her. 'It will help you to understand the problem that has—thankfully!—been presented to us.'

Faith stepped into Mrs Heavenly's vision, eager to

learn what her assignment was to be. Christmas was only two days away—always a fraught time of year for humans, when the inadequacies in their normally busy lives often became glaringly obvious. It was also a time when they often cried out for help to cope with those difficulties.

'This incident happened a short time ago,' Mrs Heavenly told her softly, a smile on her cherubic face.

Faith gazed down interestedly at the scene being enacted below them.

A tiny woman of about thirty—startlingly beautiful, her fine-boned body clothed in a black trouser suit and cream blouse, and with golden-blonde hair cropped close to her head—was stepping lithely out of a lift, her expression one of determination as she marched down the carpeted corridor to rap sharply on an oak door at the end of the hallway.

'She looks rather angry,' Faith murmured.

Mrs Heavenly nodded unconcernedly. 'She invariably is,' she informed Faith lightly.

'Why—? Goodness, who is *that*?' Faith gasped as the oak door swung open to reveal a man almost as handsome as Gabriel himself.

Or Lucifer, she decided as an afterthought. His hair was so dark it was almost black, his eyes so dark a brown it was difficult to see where the iris stopped and the pupil began. As for his looks—they could only be described as devilishly attractive.

'Is he her husband?' Faith prompted breathlessly.

'Hardly.' Mrs Heavenly smiled. 'Listen,' she encouraged softly.

* * *

'Ms Hardy,' the man greeted dryly. 'To what do I owe this unexpected pleasure?'

Olivia, despite the obvious derision in his tone, stared back at him unmovingly. Ethan Sherbourne had occupied the apartment directly above hers for over a year now. But apart from an occasional greeting to him—on the rare occasion they happened to get into the lift together—or to one of the constant stream of women that seemed to flow in and out of his apartment, Olivia had remained firmly detached from the man.

The only other exception being when his mail became confused with her own. Which it had already several times this Christmas.

'Yours, I believe.' She held up the pink envelope she carried with her.

He raised dark brows as he reached out a lean hand and took the envelope, checking the writing on the front before holding it up in front of his nose and sniffing appreciatively.

'Gwendoline,' he announced knowingly.

Olivia repressed a delicate shudder. 'I didn't realise women still did that sort of thing,' she commented scathingly.

Neither did Olivia understand why Mr Pulman, the caretaker of this exclusive apartment building, should think she might be the recipient of a scented Christmas card!

Ethan Sherbourne gave a roguish smile. 'Only certain women,' he drawled huskily.

Utterly stupid ones, in Olivia's opinion. But she was sure Ethan Sherbourne wasn't in the least interested in her opinion. She wasn't tall, willowy—or young!—as the majority of women trooping in and out of his apartment seemed to be.

She gave a cool inclination of her head. 'I'll leave you to open your card—' She broke off with a frown as the lift doors opened down the corridor, immediately releasing the ear-splitting wail of a baby. A very young baby, by the sound of it, Olivia realised, wincingly.

She turned slowly in the direction of the cry, just in time to move out of the way of the young woman striding purposefully towards Ethan Sherbourne's apartment.

The roguish smile had been wiped off Ethan Sherbourne's face the moment he looked at the approaching virago. 'Shelley...?' He betrayed his uncertainty with a frown.

The tall, youthfully leggy blonde, looking not much more than a child herself, gave him a humourless smile, the screaming baby held firmly in her arms. 'I'm surprised you remember me,' she snapped. 'We met so briefly.'

'Of course I remember you,' Ethan Sherbourne returned smoothly, sparing a reluctant glance for the shawl-wrapped bundle in the girl's arms. 'And this is...?'

Olivia stood to one side of the hallway now, an unwilling but at the same time fascinated eavesdropper on this conversation.

The girl—for, on closer inspection, she most certainly was a girl, probably no older than twenty or so—was gazing down at the screaming baby with a look that somehow managed to combine motherly love and sheer terror at the same time.

'Here.' She thrust the child into Ethan Sherbourne's unsuspecting arms.

The screaming—to its mother's obvious frustration—instantly ceased, although emotional hiccups quickly followed.

'She obviously prefers you to me, anyway,' the young woman choked tearfully—as if this was the final straw as far as she was concerned. 'Her name is Andrea. Everything she needs is in here.' She took a holdall off her shoulder and dropped it onto the floor. 'She will want feeding in about an hour. I just can't cope any more.'

With a last heart-wrenching glance at the baby she turned on her heel and ran back into the lift, desperately pressing the button to close the doors.

'Shelley—!' Ethan Sherbourne's cry of protest died in his throat as the lift doors closed on the distraught mother, followed by the sound of its descent.

At the same time his raised voice startled the baby in his arms, and it began crying again.

Its obviously distressed cry shot through Olivia's nerve-endings with the sharpness of a knife, and her face was pale as she grimaced painfully.

'Where do you think you're going?' Ethan Sherbourne demanded grimly, his voice raised above the baby's wail.

Olivia had turned, intending to follow the young mother's example and escape from the situation!

She turned back to Ethan Sherbourne, her brows raised. 'I've delivered your card—which I received by mistake.' She shrugged. 'I thought I would leave you to deal with this...second delivery of the day alone,' she explained dryly.

Dark brown eyes narrowed icily at her obvious sarcasm. 'Don't be so damned stupid,' he snapped, striding out of the apartment to move forward to the lift and press the button for its return, the pink-wrapped bundle—still crying—held awkwardly in his arms.

Olivia gave him a considering look. 'Where are *you* going?' Not too far, she didn't think; she doubted this baby was going to wait for another hour to be fed.

'After Shelley, of course.' He rasped his impatience, looking more harassed by the second. The baby's initial response to being held in his arms rather than its mother's was definitely gone for good. 'What the hell is wrong with her?' he demanded exasperatedly of Olivia.

Olivia looked stunned by the question. 'What on earth makes you think I would know?'

'You're a woman, aren't you?' Ethan's agitation was fast reaching danger level. 'At least...' his gaze moved over her trouser suit '...I presume you are. Where the hell is the damned lift?' he grated between clenched teeth.

'Maybe if you stopped swearing—'

'You think that might stop the baby screaming?' He conveyed his doubt with another frown.

'No,' Olivia answered reasonably. 'I would just prefer it if you did.'

If looks alone could kill, Olivia knew she would have been struck down in that moment. She only just stopped herself from taking a step backwards as Ethan Sherbourne took a threatening step towards her.

'Er—your lift seems finally to have arrived.' She pointed past him with some relief to the waiting elevator, its doors open invitingly.

He glanced from the open lift to Olivia, and back again. 'So it has,' he acknowledged. 'Here,' he offered.

And promptly deposited the baby into Olivia's arms!

Not welcoming arms. Not waiting. Not even willing. In fact, her initial feelings of satisfaction at one of this man's past relationships having caught up with him—with a vengeance—disappeared totally as she found *she* was the one left holding the baby!

'Mr Sherbourne—'

'I have to try and catch up with Shelley,' he told her firmly before stepping into the lift. 'Take care of the baby until I get back with her mother.'

Take care of—!

The lift doors closed, leaving Olivia alone in the hallway.

No, not alone…

A now silent baby lay in her arms, staring up at her with unblinking trust, Olivia realised as she reluctantly looked down at Andrea.

Olivia's legs began to shake, quickly followed by the rest of her body, until she knew she was actually in danger of collapsing completely. But with a very young baby in her arms that was not a good idea.

The door to Ethan Sherbourne's apartment still stood wide open. Not particularly inviting, but this baby was, after all, Ethan's responsibility.

Olivia managed to reach one of the armchairs in the ultra-modern lounge before her legs collapsed beneath her. But only just. She was shaking all over, her breath coming in short, hyperventilating gasps.

How dared Ethan Sherbourne do this to her?

How *dared* he?

* * *

'Mr Sherbourne is certainly in need of a little divine intervention,' Faith murmured sympathetically as the vision in the apartment stilled.

Mrs Heavenly straightened, shaking her head. 'Mr Sherbourne isn't the one requesting our help, my dear.'

Faith blinked. 'Well, of course Shelley is very troubled—obviously overwhelmed by motherhood—No?' She frowned as Mrs Heavenly shook her head again. 'Surely not baby Andrea...? No, of course not,' she answered herself. 'But that only leaves...'

'Olivia,' Mrs Heavenly confirmed with satisfaction. 'Yes, my dear, it's Olivia Hardy who needs our help this Christmas.'

Faith glanced back to the woman stilled in the frame. Beautiful, and obviously successful, as she lived in such a luxurious apartment building; in what way, Faith wondered, did such a woman need the help of one of Mrs Heavenly's angels?

CHAPTER TWO

FAITH continued to look at the frozen vision of Olivia. 'I don't understand,' she said after some time had elapsed. 'Olivia appears to have everything going for her.'

Mrs Heavenly gave a sad shake of her head. 'Appearances can sometimes be deceptive, my dear.'

'But she is successful in her career?'

'Very. Junior partner in a very prestigious law firm.'

'And beautiful, by earthly standards, too.' Faith studied the image before her; to her Olivia looked very beautiful indeed. 'Is she married?'

'No,' Mrs Heavenly answered slowly. 'Nor does she have any children.' She pre-empted what she thought might be Faith's next question.

'Ah,' the young angel murmured with satisfaction.

'Nor does she *want* a husband or children,' Mrs Heavenly added pointedly.

Faith felt more puzzled than ever. 'But she has asked for our help?'

'Oh, yes.' Mrs Heavenly sighed her satisfaction. 'For the first time in ten years Olivia has sent up a prayer. And I don't intend letting this opportunity pass us by.'

Faith felt no nearer to knowing in exactly what way Olivia Hardy needed their help, but she trusted Mrs Heavenly's instincts implicitly. If she said Olivia Hardy had not only asked for help but was also deserving of it, that was good enough for Faith. If only she knew in what way she *could* help...!

'Watch what happens next,' Mrs Heavenly invited as she saw Faith's continued confusion.

The frame in the vision instantly shifted, and the sound came back too—the tiny baby was hiccupping again in between drawing in shuddering breaths.

Olivia looked down at the tiny being in her arms. The baby, although still very young, looked well cared for; her cheeks were round, her skin a healthy pink, and her blue eyes gazed back unfocused at Olivia.

The pink blanket Andrea was wrapped in was clean, and she wore a pretty pink woollen suit beneath, plus a matching hat that hid the colour of her hair. If she had any!

'You're going to get too hot in all this wool, aren't you, poppet?' Olivia spoke gently to the baby even as she eased herself up out of the chair to lie Andrea down on the thickly carpeted floor and began slowly unwrapping her.

Almost like a Christmas present—except a baby was the very last thing Olivia wanted, for Christmas or at any other time!

The hair beneath the woollen hat, Olivia discovered a few seconds later, was a startling black. Exactly like her father's, she realised with a disapproving tightening of her mouth.

She wasn't a prude, by any means—in her career it was best not to be! But Shelley had looked no older than twenty at most—possibly even younger than that—and Ethan Sherbourne, although very attractive in a devilish sort of way, and obviously physically fit, was a man in his early forties. And, from the little Shelley had said before her abrupt departure, the relationship between the two of them had been so fleeting the young girl had been doubtful that Ethan Sherbourne would even remember her!

To Olivia this whole situation seemed just so irresponsible. It was also one that could easily have been avoided. In her opinion, Ethan Sherbourne, with his obvious maturity, should have been the one to avoid it!

Selfish, Olivia instantly decided. Totally lacking in thought for anyone but himself and his own pleasure. He lived here, in sumptuous luxury, with a harem of women at his beck and call, while a young girl like Shelley, obviously not in the same financial bracket at all, by the look of her worn clothing, was left to bring up her child—and Ethan Sherbourne's!—completely on her own. It was men like him who—

'She had already disappeared by the time I got downstairs.' A disgruntled Ethan Sherbourne strode forcefully into the apartment, slamming the door behind him.

'Why didn't you just follow her back to her home?' Olivia reasoned—it was what she had expected him to do, after all.

'For the simple reason that I have no idea where she lives!' He scowled darkly at Olivia as she stood up with the baby held in her arms, now minus her blanket, hat and woollen outer suit. The pink Babygro that she wore beneath was slightly too large for her. 'How old do you think she is?' Ethan frowned.

Olivia raised blonde brows, already disgusted enough by the fact that he had no idea where Shelley lived without this too! 'Don't you know?' After all, if the relationship had been as fleeting as Shelley had implied it was, then it shouldn't be too difficult for Ethan Sherbourne to take a guess at his daughter's age!

'I would hardly have asked if I already knew, now, would I?' he snapped, moving to the array of drinks that stood on the side dresser, pouring out a large measure of whisky into one of the glasses and taking a large swallow before holding the decanter up in invitation to Olivia.

'No, thank you,' she refused coldly; she didn't think his getting drunk was going to help the situation at all!

'Suit yourself.' He shrugged before downing the rest of the whisky in the glass. 'At a guess, I would say she's somewhere between two and four months old,' he decided.

Perhaps not so fleeting a relationship, after all. Certainly not the one-night-stand that Olivia had been imagining. 'Her name is Andrea,' she bit out caustically. 'And I would agree—she's about three months old.'

Ethan's mouth twisted scornfully. 'In your expert opinion?'

Olivia drew in a sharp breath at his insulting tone. 'Now, look, Mr Sherbourne—'

'Oh, for goodness' sake, call me Ethan,' he retorted impatiently. 'After all, with Shelley's abrupt departure, we seem to have been left joint custodians of a very young baby!'

'*We* most certainly have not!' Olivia walked determinedly across the room, putting the baby firmly into Ethan's arms. 'In her mother's absence, Andrea is one hundred per cent *your* responsibility.' She stepped back pointedly. 'And, as such, I think you should be aware of the fact that Andrea needs her nappy changed,' she added with satisfaction. 'It's probably the reason she's so upset,' she guessed shrewdly.

Ethan raised the tiny baby slightly, his nose wrinkling with distaste at the obvious aroma that came up to greet him.

'I presume her nappies are in the bag—along with her food.' Olivia moved to pick up the shoulder-bag Shelley had dropped earlier, unzipping it to find everything in there that baby Andrea would need for an indefinite stay: several changes of clothes, uncountable nappies, and enough formula and bottles to feed her for a week. 'Here.' She handed Ethan one of the tiny disposable nappies, wipes, and barrier cream, and was completely unsympathetic as he tried to balance those as well as hold the baby.

Dark brown eyes opened wide. 'You expect me to change Andrea's nappy?' he said with obvious disbelief.

'*I* don't expect you to do anything,' Olivia assured him lightly. 'But I think Shelley does!'

Ethan gave up all pretence of holding on to the things she had just handed him, dropping them—but fortunately not the baby!—onto the carpeted floor. 'Well, let me inform you—and Shelley too, if she were here—'

'I think that's probably the appropriate word—*if*

Shelley were here,' Olivia said sweetly. 'Which she isn't. Which only leaves you—'

'And you,' he pounced quickly.

'No way.' Olivia shook her head decisively. 'Shelley obviously believes you are more than capable of caring for Andrea.' Although in the same circumstances Olivia didn't believe she would have been so positive! 'I suggest you start fulfilling that belief by changing the baby's nappy.'

Those dark brown eyes looked at her suspiciously. 'You're enjoying this, aren't you?' he finally said slowly.

When it came to the distressing circumstances of Shelley being put in a position where she didn't know where else to turn to for help—no. But the fact that this arrogant Casanova had finally been given his comeuppance—yes, she was enjoying that!

Ethan Sherbourne was everything Olivia disliked in a man: arrogant, self-satisfied, too good-looking for his own and everyone else's good. And on today's evidence—totally amoral.

'What I happen to think about this situation isn't important,' she dismissed. 'Making the baby comfortable is, however. I'll just get a towel from the bathroom for you to lie her down on.' Which she did with no trouble whatsoever—the lay-out to this apartment was exactly the same as her own on the floor below. 'There.' She doubled the dark blue towel, placing it on the floor before looking expectantly at Ethan Sherbourne.

His cheeks were flushed as he scowled back at her darkly. 'I am not—' The baby began to cry once again. 'Maybe I am,' he muttered between clenched teeth, before moving down onto his knees and lying the baby gently down on the towel. 'How do I get into this thing?' He pulled ineffectually at the Babygro, turning the baby from side to side in his effort to find an opening.

'There are usually poppers on the insides of the legs— Oh, for goodness' sake…!' Olivia showed her impatience as he lifted the baby's legs to the left and then the right, almost turning the poor little thing over onto her face in the process. 'She's a baby, not a sack of potatoes!' Olivia bit out as she dropped down onto her knees beside him.

'Sacks of potatoes only need opening and the contents peeling—not having their nappies changed,' Ethan muttered with distaste as Olivia easily released the hidden poppers and freed the baby from the lower half of the all-in-one garment before moving out of the way. The pungent aroma was much stronger now. 'I can't believe I'm doing this,' he said a few minutes later, the soiled nappy discarded, one of the wipes held gingerly in his hand.

Olivia felt it diplomatic to take the nappy to the kitchen and dispose of it at that moment. Mainly because she didn't think Ethan Sherbourne would appreciate seeing her bent over in hysterical laughter—at his expense!

He had looked so ridiculous kneeling there on the carpet, wearing what looked to be—and probably was!—a black silk shirt and tailored black trousers, as a happy Andrea blew bubbles up at him, her joyfully kicking legs making it difficult for him to finish what he had started.

If one of his harem could only see him now—if *all* of them could see him now—they might not be quite so available to him!

That thought had the effect of sobering Olivia, if nothing else. She washed her hands before returning to the sitting room, and came to an abrupt halt as she saw Andrea was still minus her nappy while Ethan Sherbourne lay on the carpet beside her, copying her bubble-blowing antics.

Olivia felt a sudden tightness in her chest. Ethan didn't look so ridiculous any more. In fact he looked as if he was definitely enjoying himself.

He glanced across at Olivia as he sensed her standing there, his expression softened from playing with the baby. 'She's beautiful, isn't she?' he said huskily.

Olivia didn't even glance at the contented baby. 'All babies are beautiful, Mr Sherbourne,' she told him hardily.

'I thought I asked you to call me Ethan,' he reminded her softly. 'And you are…?'

'Olivia,' she provided stiffly, knowing it would be completely churlish to refuse to give him her first name—as well as non-productive; he only had to ask Mr Pulman for it if he really wanted to know.

'Olivia Hardy,' Ethan repeated mockingly as he sat up to look at her with laughing brown eyes. 'It sounds like one half of a comedy duo!'

Angry colour darkened her cheeks. 'In the circumstances, what does that make you?' she returned scathingly. 'If you'll excuse me,' she added abruptly, before he could come out with some clever reply, 'I have some case notes I need to go over this evening.' She moved towards the door, anxious to escape now.

'Of course,' he agreed, standing up. 'You're a lawyer, aren't you? Exactly what sort of lawyer?' He followed her over to the door, standing in the doorway as she stood waiting for the lift to arrive.

'A good one,' Olivia came back derisively, glancing back at him in surprise as she heard him chuckle.

'I'll just bet you are too,' he replied appreciatively. 'Olivia—' He broke off as the sound of the baby whimpering could be heard behind him.

Olivia's mouth thinned humourlessly. 'I believe that is your cue to feed her,' she told him as she stepped inside the lift. 'Good luck!'

Ethan grimaced. 'I think Andrea is going to need that more than I am!'

He was probably right, Olivia decided as the lift began its descent. Sorry as she felt for Shelley in her obvious desperation, she couldn't help thinking that the other woman should have chosen someone with more competence at the task than Ethan Sherbourne obviously had. Even though, as Andrea's father, a more appropriate minder couldn't be found!

As she let herself into her own silent apartment she could still hear the baby's cries, whether real or imagined, so she moved to switch on the television and drown out the noise—instantly turning the volume down as she realised she was probably the one responsible for disturbing the neighbours now! Besides, no matter how loud the television, it didn't stop Olivia from worrying about the baby.

Would Ethan Sherbourne know how to feed Andrea

properly? Did he know how to make up the formula? To use sterilised water and not some straight from the tap? To tell if the milk was the right temperature for Andrea to drink? That he had to wind the baby after every ounce or so to prevent her getting tummy ache?

Olivia switched off the television impatiently, striding through to her bathroom to turn on the shower before going into the adjoining bedroom to undress. A shower might help to relax her. Anything to take her mind off what might be going wrong in the apartment above her.

Except that it didn't.

She stood under the punishing jet of the power shower for over ten minutes, desperately trying to channel her thoughts into the case she was working on at the moment. And failing miserably. How could she possibly think of work after the disturbing sequence of events earlier this evening?

Finally she came back through to her bedroom, wearing a peach-coloured silk robe, and looked around her appreciatively at the lovely things she had bought to surround and calm her. It was all the best that money could buy: a Mediterranean-style kitchen, antique furniture in every room, brocade drapes at the windows, luxuriously sumptuous carpets on the floors, several original paintings hanging on the cream-coloured walls.

And yet as Olivia looked around her she knew that it wasn't enough. That it never had been...

She sat down on the side of the bed, knowing exactly what she was going to do now and powerless to stop herself.

The photograph lay in the bottom drawer of her bedside cabinet—the only thing in that particular drawer. Her hand shook slightly as she picked it up, the tears streaming hotly down her cheeks even before she looked down at the picture.

Oh, God, Olivia pleaded emotionally, please, please help me to get through this!

CHAPTER THREE

'WHAT…?' Faith moved slightly in an effort to see the subject in the photograph Olivia held, only to be disappointed as Olivia suddenly clasped it against her chest, those tears still falling down the paleness of her cheeks.

Mrs Heavenly straightened, moving a hand gently over the vision and instantly dispersing the images into a wispy cloud. 'As you can see, Olivia's prayer is for help to get through Christmas.' She smiled at Faith. 'Not too difficult an assignment, I would have thought.'

Faith looked searchingly at her mentor. That wasn't exactly what Olivia had prayed for…

'So there you have it, my dear,' Mrs Heavenly told her brightly, shuffling some papers on her desk. 'The scene is already set for you to be able to do that quite easily. It's just a question of continuing to bring Olivia and Ethan together—'

'Ethan Sherbourne?' Faith couldn't hide her surprise. 'But isn't he—?'

'Ethan isn't exactly what he seems,' Mrs Heavenly assured her kindly. 'In fact, he could do with a little divine intervention himself! But I think on this occasion it might be better if… Don't be too visible, my dear,' she encouraged Faith. 'Neither Olivia nor Ethan are…well, shall we say that neither of them is particularly…a believer?'

Was it her imagination, Faith wondered, or did Mrs Heavenly's gaze no longer quite meet her own…?

Ridiculous, she instantly answered herself. Mrs Heavenly was the most open-hearted of all the—

'Poor Ethan.' Mrs Heavenly had opened the vision once again, was shaking her head regretfully as she looked down. 'Although he does seem to be coping well, in the circumstances,' she commented admiringly. 'Perhaps now would be a good time, Faith…?'

'Of course.' Faith drew herself out of the speculative trance she had lapsed into. 'Time I was going,' she agreed.

'But remember, Faith!' Mrs Heavenly called out to her before she disappeared. 'No matter what other distractions might occur, Olivia is the subject of your assignment.'

'I'll remember,' Faith assured her softly as she floated down to Earth.

And she *would* remember. But that didn't mean she couldn't try and be of some help to Shelley and Andrea while she was about it. Possibly even to Ethan Sherbourne too…

The photograph was back in its drawer and Olivia was wearing grey silk pyjamas. Her dinner of smoked salmon and salad was on the glass-topped dining table with a glass of white wine at exactly the right temperature for drinking, when a loud knocking on the door interrupted the calm enjoyment of her meal.

Who on earth—?

The wailing of a distressed baby penetrated the thickness of the door to her apartment, the tranquillity she had so determinedly made for herself instantly shattered.

Ethan Sherbourne and his—and baby Andrea, Olivia instantly realised. What could possible have gone wrong now?

Whatever it was, she knew she couldn't just ignore that cry; Ethan Sherbourne could stew in his own juice, as far as she was concerned, but the baby was another matter entirely.

'What have you done to her now?' Olivia demanded as she wrenched the door open—only to find herself staring into an empty hallway!

But how—? What—? She had been so sure...

She had to have been mistaken; there was no way Ethan could have knocked at her apartment and then disappeared back into the lift before she opened the door. Besides, what would be the point of him doing such a thing?

Olivia shook her head dazedly, closing the door to walk slowly back into her dining room.

She barely had time to sit back down and take a sip of her wine before that knock sounded on the door a second time. The crying of the baby was slightly fainter this time, but still audible to Olivia's acute hearing nonetheless.

She stood, striding angrily over to the door this time. This evening had already been traumatic enough; she was decidedly not in the mood to play childish games with Ethan Sherbourne!

'What on earth do you think you're playing at...?' Olivia's angry tirade trailed off abruptly as she opened the door and found the corridor empty again, a glance up and down the hallway showing her that there really was no one there.

Well, she wasn't going to give Ethan Sherbourne the chance to play this childish prank on her a third time. It wasn't in the least funny, and she intended telling Ethan Sherbourne so!

It took her exactly two minutes to throw off her silk pyjamas, pull on designer denims and a loose black shirt and slip her bare feet into a pair of loafers, before marching determinedly out of her apartment. She got into the lift, pressing the button for the next floor and stepping out to stride forcefully down the corridor and put her finger on Ethan Sherbourne's doorbell. And kept it on. Two could play at this game!

Ethan opened the door and barely had time to raise surprised brows before Olivia pushed him firmly to one side and strode into his apartment.

She looked anxiously around the sitting room, finally turning a blazing grey gaze on Ethan Sherbourne as he stood just inside the room, curiously returning her gaze. 'What have you done to her?' Olivia demanded coldly. 'And don't tell me nothing,' she added impatiently, before he had time to answer, 'because I could hear her crying all the way downstairs!'

'I doubt that very much,' Ethan drawled as he walked further into the room. 'The only reason I bought this apartment was because I was assured by the agent that the building is completely soundproof.'

Olivia snorted softly to herself. No doubt he had been thinking of his harem at the time!

'I don't care what you were assured,' she returned. 'I definitely heard her crying.'

'I presume by "her" that you mean Andrea?' He derisively turned the tables on her after her earlier comment to him. 'And exactly what do you *think* I've done to her?' He folded his arms across his chest as he faced Olivia, his expression deceptively calm as he looked at her with mild curiosity.

Grey eyes flashed warningly as Olivia glared back at him. 'How should I know?' she replied shortly. 'Judging from previous evidence of your ability to know the needs of a young baby, you've probably tried to feed her steak or something equally unsuitable!' She looked around the room for a second time. 'Where is she?'

'Changed. Fed. Played with. Fast asleep.' He continued to look at Olivia, now with amusement.

'But I heard her,' Olivia said restlessly. 'I definitely heard her crying.' Although she equally definitely couldn't hear the baby crying now…

Ethan slowly shook his head. 'I don't think so.'

'Then where is she?' Olivia was low on patience at the best of times—at the moment it was non-existent!

He sighed, dropping his arms down to his sides. 'If you promise to be quiet, I'll show you.' He raised dark, questioning brows.

Her cheeks flushed fiery-red. 'Of course I'll be quiet,' she clipped. 'What—?'

'If you'll excuse my saying so, you haven't shown much sign of it in the last few minutes,' Ethan observed.

Olivia had been about to question him sharply again, but at these words her lips clamped together. Although she couldn't resist another glare in Ethan's direction.

'Better.' Ethan gave a mocking inclination of his head. 'Follow me through to my bedroom.'

Under other circumstances Olivia would have told him exactly what he could do with such an invitation. But in her concern for Andrea she resisted any such response, instead following Ethan into the bedroom situated directly above her own, lit by a low-voltage lamp on the bedside table.

What looked suspiciously like a drawer lay in the middle of the sumptuous king-size bed, and nestled securely inside that drawer, covered with a many-times-folded satin sheet, lay baby Andrea, looking absolutely adorable as she slept contentedly.

Also looking as if she had been like that for some time...

'Satisfied?' Ethan asked softly at Olivia's side.

She swallowed hard, nodding wordlessly. Whoever she had heard crying a few minutes ago, it obviously hadn't been Andrea.

In the circumstances, Olivia felt very reluctant to mention those two knocks on her apartment door which had accompanied the sound of crying...

'That was—the idea of a drawer for a bed—it was very inventive,' she told Ethan awkwardly once they had returned to the sitting-room.

Ethan eyed her wryly, 'Didn't you think I could be inventive?'

Her cheeks coloured heatedly at his obvious double meaning. 'To be honest, I've never given the matter any thought!' she assured him quickly.

'Stay for a drink now you're here?' he asked, moving to the array of drinks on the dresser.

Olivia thought longingly of her uneaten dinner, her rapidly warming glass of white wine. But her continuing concern for Andrea—despite the fact that Ethan seemed to be proving better at baby-minding than she would ever have imagined!—was of much greater importance at this particular moment.

She deliberately ignored the offer of a drink. Socialising with a man like Ethan Sherbourne was definitely not on her Christmas list of things still to do! 'What are you going to do about Andrea?' she asked.

'"Do" about her?' Ethan repeated softly.

Olivia frowned. 'Well, you can't just keep her here!'

'Why can't I?'

'Because—well, because—' Olivia's exasperation was such that she could hardly speak.

'What else do you suggest I do with her, Olivia? Call the authorities? Have her taken into care, over Christmas of all times? Cause all sorts of unnecessary complications for Shelley once she realises what she's done and comes back to reclaim her baby?' He shook his head, pouring red wine into two glasses, his expression grim as he held one of those glasses out to Olivia. 'Or perhaps you intend informing the authorities yourself?' he added harshly. 'Part of your duties as a responsible lawyer—?'

'Don't be ridiculous!' Olivia cut in instantly, drawing in a long, controlling breath. 'I have no wish to make this situation any worse for Shelley. I just don't think—'

'That I'm capable of looking after Andrea?' Ethan interrupted challengingly.

How could she possibly claim that when he had already more than proved that he was?

'No, it isn't that.' She sighed irritably. 'I just— I don't drink red wine!' She put her glass down untouched as she realised she had taken it from him without realising what she was doing.

'Pity. Apart from the odd emergency—like earlier,' he drawled, 'I drink very little else but red wine.' He straightened. 'So, you agree with me that until Shelley returns to claim Andrea she stays here with me?'

She hadn't said that at all! His lifestyle—days spent in his apartment being visited by a string of beautiful women, evenings and weekends spent with whoever— was not compatible with caring for the young baby that Andrea was.

But what was the alternative…?

Besides, there was one other important factor in this scenario—he was the baby's father.

'Unless you have any other ideas about what I should do?' Ethan prompted smoothly.

Olivia frowned at the question. 'Me?'

'Yes—you,' Ethan echoed mockingly. 'You could offer to care for Andrea yourself. Although I suppose a baby would mess up your sterile lifestyle.'

Olivia bristled angrily at this last remark. 'And what about *your* lifestyle?' she flew back. 'Exactly how do you intend explaining away baby Andrea's presence to your other—*friends*? Friends like Gwendoline of the perfumed Christmas card,' she reminded him as he would have spoken. 'Not with the truth, I'm sure,' she added.

'You think that wouldn't go down too well…?' Ethan asked thoughtfully.

Not unless those other women were completely stupid—no! But then, Olivia had no evidence to prove that they weren't exactly that! A couple of them had even been chatting and laughing together beside Olivia in the lift one day as they went up to his apartment.

'This is ridiculous!' she exclaimed. 'I only came up here—'

'Yes—why did you come up here?' Ethan put in huskily.

Her gaze faltered at that throaty tone in his voice. 'I told you. I heard Andrea crying—'

'And I have since proved to you that you couldn't have done,' he drawled. 'After I had changed her I warmed a bottle and fed her. Then I tickled her toes and played with her for a while before she fell into an exhausted sleep in my arms. She's stayed asleep for at least the last hour,' he ended firmly.

Olivia didn't dwell on thoughts of his playing with Andrea; it didn't quite fit in with the mental image she had of him…

But his claim did make a total nonsense of those two knocks on her apartment door earlier and the sound of a baby crying!

And if it hadn't been Ethan knocking on the door, or Andrea crying, then who—or what?—had she heard…?

Maybe she hadn't really heard anything? Maybe it

had just been her imagination, after all? If that were the case, then this Christmas promised to be even harder to get through than all the others had been!

And it was obvious from Ethan Sherbourne's sceptical expression that he believed she had used the claim as an excuse to come back up here to his apartment!

Arrogant, conceited pig!

'Obviously, as you say, I was mistaken,' she answered him frostily. 'I'm sorry to have disturbed you.'

'Oh, don't apologise, Olivia,' he replied softly. 'I've rather enjoyed being disturbed by you!'

He probably had too, Olivia realised impotently.

'Goodnight!' she said suddenly, turning sharply on her heel and leaving before he had the chance to say anything else facetious.

The man was nothing but a womaniser. Even with his own illegitimate daughter in his apartment he hadn't been able to resist the impulse to flirt with her!

Olivia hoped the baby kept him awake all night!

It had been too soon, Faith decided as she looked at Olivia's face when she re-entered her apartment, easily able to gauge Olivia's mood as one of complete antagonism towards Ethan Sherbourne.

Oh, well, there was Christmas Eve to go yet— Christmas Day, too. And miracles had been worked before in much less time than that.

Besides, Olivia's brief absence from her apartment had given Faith the opportunity to take a look at that photograph Olivia kept hidden away in the bottom drawer of her bedside cabinet.

Faith only hoped Mrs Heavenly hadn't been watching—her mentor might see her behaviour as cheating!

CHAPTER FOUR

OLIVIA felt absolutely exhausted as she made her way home on Christmas Eve.

Her client had decided, after Olivia had worked on her case for weeks, to reconcile with her husband, and as such had no further need to sort out the custody of their child. The fact that the reconciliation would probably only last as long as Christmas—maybe as long as New Year if the couple were lucky—meant that Olivia would have to restart the exhausting business of pinning down the husband as soon as her office reopened in January. Not exactly a good way to end a year's work!

The office party had also taken place this afternoon and early evening. It was an event Olivia usually tried her best to avoid, but she had been prevented from doing so this year by a personal request from one of the senior partners.

'Not good for company morale not to have the management in evidence,' was how Dennis had put it—when all he had really wanted was the legitimate excuse of Christmas mistletoe to try and kiss her. If one of them—she wasn't sure who—hadn't inadvertently knocked some files off the top of a cabinet, thus diverting attention from the fraught situation, Olivia was very much afraid she would have had to slap him on the face!

Yet another situation she would have to sort out when she returned to work in the New Year, she acknowledged with a sigh. Not that there was anything wrong with Dennis; he was only about ten years older than she was, single, attractive, and had made it more than obvious to her over the last few months that he was very available. She just wasn't interested.

Rushing to the local supermarket when she had finally managed to escape—conscious of the fact that the larger shops would be closed for the following three days—and having to fight her way through frantic last-minute shoppers for the few fresh provisions she would need to see her through that time had been the final straw for Olivia in what had already been a disastrous day.

She just wanted to close her apartment door on the rest of the world, pour herself a glass of chilled white wine, put her feet up on the sofa as she drank it—and hope that she could somehow avoid even knowing it was Christmas!

The first, second, and even the third of those needs was soon satisfied. But the knock on her door, even as she sat back on the sofa with a contented sigh, seemed to imply that the fourth one wasn't going to be quite so easy…

Especially when she opened the door to find Ethan Sherbourne standing outside, with baby Andrea reclining in a baby buggy, deep blue eyes wide open as she looked about her curiously.

Olivia's gaze rose slowly from the baby to centre questioningly on Ethan Sherbourne.

He smiled. 'I went shopping for a few things today that I thought I might need,' he explained.

Olivia was curious as to how he had done that with baby Andrea in tow, but determinedly didn't ask the question. She did not want to know any more about this situation than she needed to. Did not want to become involved!

'You look tired.' Ethan looked down at her concernedly. 'Had a tough day?'

Olivia gave a startled blink, feeling the sudden rush of unwanted tears as they stung her eyes. It had just been so long since anyone had asked her how her day had been, let alone noticed how tired she looked...!

She swallowed hard, pushing the momentary weakness to the back of her mind. 'Probably not as tough as yours,' she allowed dryly, standing firmly in the doorway. She did not intend inviting him—or Andrea!—inside.

In the time she had lived in this apartment building Olivia could probably count on one hand the amount of times she had actually seen or spoken to Ethan Sherbourne. Even then it had only usually been as the two of them had passed, either going in or out of the lift. In the last twenty-four hours she had seen him almost as many times as in the whole of the previous year—and spoken to him far too much for her liking!

Ethan shrugged now. 'It really wasn't that bad. Andrea is still at that stage where she sleeps more than she's awake.'

He didn't exactly look frazzled, Olivia had to

admit—in fact, he looked in better condition than she did!

Once again she wondered what the man actually did for a living. He obviously hadn't been at work today if he had been shopping and looking after Andrea all day.

'What can I do for you?' Olivia prompted sharply.

Ethan was wearing a jacket over his silk shirt and tailored trousers—looked, in fact, as if he was on his way out...

'It isn't for me,' he answered smoothly. 'It's for Andrea. You see—'

'The answer is no,' Olivia cut in, before he could even finish what he wanted to say. He *was* dressed to go out, damn him! 'Most definitely no,' she repeated firmly. 'I've only just got in, and I haven't even had a chance to eat dinner yet. I was going to take a long, leisurely bath before—'

'Settling down for the evening,' Ethan pounced with a triumphant grin, pushing the buggy inside her apartment and running one of the wheels over Olivia's toes in the process. 'There's absolutely no reason why you can't still take that long, leisurely bath—Andrea is far too young to look and tell!' he pronounced suggestively. 'She's just been bathed, fed and changed too, so—'

'Is it me?' Olivia followed him through to her sitting room, completely exasperated with his railroading behaviour. 'Or have I just told you that I'm busy?'

'I have to go out, Olivia,' Ethan interrupted, his teasing tone of a few seconds ago completely gone. 'And I can't take Andrea with me.' He answered what he had guessed—correctly—was going to be her next question.

'Why can't you?' She glared at him. But from the way he was dressed she already knew the answer to that; the particular member of the harem he was meeting this evening wouldn't understand about baby Andrea!

His gaze shifted slightly, no longer quite meeting hers. 'I would really rather not say.'

Olivia's eyes widened incredulously. 'You would really rather not—? Now, you just listen here, Ethan Sherbourne—'

'I would love to, Olivia—but I'm already late for my appointment.' He handed her the bag he had slung over his shoulder before bending to kiss her lightly on the cheek. 'I promise not to be late,' he told her on a teasing note.

'Ethan—' Olivia gasped—only to discover she was already talking to herself. Ethan had closed the apartment door softly behind him as he left.

Leaving her alone with baby Andrea for goodness knew how long. Olivia gave absolutely no credence to Ethan's claim that he wouldn't be late.

She just couldn't believe he had done this to her!

Or that he had kissed her...!

She raised a hand to touch her cheek, surprised to see that her hand was shaking slightly. And her cheek felt as if it were burning.

Dennis Carter had tried to kiss her fully on the lips earlier, tried to grab hold of her behind a filing cabinet, and all she had felt was revulsion. Ethan Sherbourne merely kissed her on the cheek and she was quivering like a schoolgirl.

Which just went to prove she was more in need of that leisurely bath and quiet dinner than she had realised. Ethan Sherbourne had gone out to spend the evening with one of his legion of women-friends, literally leaving Olivia holding the baby, and she was standing here in a daze because the damn man had had the nerve to kiss her on the cheek.

Too much cheap wine at the office party. That had to be the answer.

A slight whimper from Andrea brought Olivia back to a complete awareness of her predicament. Whether either of them liked it or not, it seemed they were stuck with each other—at least for several hours.

Olivia went down on her haunches beside the buggy. 'I'm not at all happy about being abandoned by Ethan in this way myself,' she assured the baby wryly. 'But learn from this experience, poppet.'

She reached out and gently touched one of Andrea's tiny hands. Her baby fingers immediately clenched about one of Olivia's own. 'We're both left sitting at home while your daddy goes out.' She tried to get up, suddenly finding herself unable to move as Andrea continued to hang on to her finger. 'That's it, poppet.' She smiled. 'We women have to stick together, don't we? How about we go into the kitchen now, to prepare me some dinner?'

She gently released her finger before straightening to wheel the buggy through to the adjoining room.

She found herself chattering away to the baby as she moved about the kitchen, sitting at the breakfast bar to eat her food rather than going through to the dining room as she usually did because Andrea seemed absolutely fascinated by the array of shining pots and pans suspended from the rack in the middle of the kitchen ceiling.

She really was the most adorable baby, Olivia decided as she watched Andrea yawn tiredly before falling back into a contented sleep.

Whatever trauma had occurred in Andrea's life in the last twenty-four hours—her mother's desperate flight, then being cared for by the inexperienced Ethan Sherbourne, and now being left with yet another complete stranger—Andrea remained impervious to it all, completely unaware anything was wrong in her young life. Or that she wasn't completely loved and cared for.

Not so Olivia, whose heart ached for this helpless little being as she wondered what on earth the future would hold for her.

Andrea, like all babies, deserved to be loved by her mother *and* her father—to be brought up and loved in as stable a homelife as possible. Even if—as in this case—her parents chose not to live together. Somehow Olivia couldn't see this being so for Andrea.

Once again Olivia felt the tears falling hotly down her cheeks. Tears that she hadn't cried for so long. Tears she hadn't allowed herself to cry.

Damn Ethan Sherbourne for involving her in the mess he had made of his life! And double damn him for just leaving the baby here with her like this!

When he returned—from the arms of whatever woman he was spending the evening with!—she was going to tell him exactly what she thought of him.

Exactly!

* * *

'How's it going?' Mrs Heavenly enquired interestedly as Faith stood before her.

Faith sighed. 'Slowly.'

'Tomorrow is Christmas Day,' the elderly angel reminded her gently.

Faith was well aware what day tomorrow was. And she had been doing everything she could to try and bring about a miracle for Olivia. But it was rather difficult when Olivia herself—despite having asked for help—was so adamantly against finding happiness.

Look at the way she had behaved with that lovely Dennis Carter at the office party earlier. The poor man was completely besotted with her, had apparently been inviting her out to dinner with him for months, and today he had finally plucked up the courage to kiss her—and look what had happened.

From the angry gleam in Olivia's eyes following that attempted kiss, what would have happened if Faith hadn't chosen to knock some files onto the floor and thus divert Olivia's attention was that Olivia would actually have slapped the poor man. And goodness knew, as Dennis was effectively one of Olivia's bosses, what the repercussions of that might have been!

Faith gave another sigh. 'Olivia is—a little difficult,' she said, with understatement.

Mrs Heavenly gave a sympathetic smile. 'No one said this job was easy!'

'No,' Faith agreed slowly.

'What are they all doing now?' The cherubic face looked up at her enquiringly.

'Ethan has gone out. I have no idea where,' Faith

reported. 'Olivia has fed Andrea, and the two of them are now fast asleep.'

'I see.' Mrs Heavenly looked serious. 'How do Olivia and Ethan seem together now?'

Faith pulled a face. 'It's a little difficult to tell— Olivia is either furiously angry with him or else she's in tears.' She shook her head. 'I don't—'

'In tears?' Mrs Heavenly echoed softly. 'Olivia has cried again since we saw her yesterday?'

'Buckets,' Faith confirmed reluctantly, totally astounded when Mrs Heavenly gave her one of her beaming smiles. 'What—?'

'Whatever you're doing, Faith, it seems to be working.' The elderly angel nodded her satisfaction. 'But I would get back down there now, if I were you,' she advised quickly. 'Ethan is standing outside Olivia's apartment about to knock on her door.'

'The mood she was in before she fell asleep in the chair, she's likely to have an axe in her hands when she answers that knock!' Faith opined, before quickly making her descent.

Hopefully she would be in time to prevent Olivia from actually using that axe!

CHAPTER FIVE

'AND just where do you think you have been till almost midnight?' Olivia demanded to know as she opened the door to face Ethan Sherbourne, having glanced at the clock to check the time before answering his knock.

Ethan raised dark brows before glancing down at the gold watch on his wrist. 'Eleven-thirty-one is hardly midnight,' he returned calmly.

'It's hardly early, either—' She broke off her tirade as Ethan grinned at her unconcernedly, darkly frowning her irritation at his reaction. 'And just what is so funny?' she snapped, not in the best of moods anyway, after being woken from her dreamless sleep.

'It's just that I haven't had someone tell me off for being late home for more years than I care to think about.' His grin turned to a throaty chuckle. 'It's rather nice,' he added wistfully.

'Nice!' Olivia echoed incredulously. 'What on earth could possible by "nice" about being shouted at because you're late home?' Really, the man was even more exasperating than she had previously realised.

Ethan smiled ruefully. 'That someone cares enough to mention the fact, I suppose.'

Olivia drew in a sharp breath. 'It isn't a question of caring, Ethan,' she assured him. 'I am merely bringing it to your attention because it's well past time you took Andrea home for the night!'

'Where is she, by the way?' Ethan glanced past Olivia into her quiet and seemingly deserted apartment.

'After the speed with which you left earlier, I'm surprised you care,' she scorned.

His smile instantly faded, dark eyes suddenly intense as he looked at her. 'Believe me, Olivia, I care.'

The softness of his tone, the conviction behind his words, was enough to make her blush uncomfortably; after all, the situation behind Andrea's birth was still all guesswork on her part. 'Andrea is fast asleep in my bedroom,' she assured him quietly, holding the door open wider for him to enter. 'I'll take you through—'

'Leave it for a moment,' Ethan rasped before dropping down into one of her armchairs, suddenly looking very tired. 'This has been a very fraught evening,' he said heavily.

The word *good* instantly sprang into Olivia's mind. If he chose to go out with one of his women instead of facing up to his responsibility towards Andrea, then he deserved—

'I've seen Shelley this evening, Olivia,' Ethan continued wearily. 'If you wouldn't mind, I would like to tell you about it.'

Olivia was absolutely stunned to learn she had completely misunderstood the reason for his disappearance this evening. Not only that, she was also taken aback that he actually wanted to talk to *her* about it.

But did she want to know? Did she want to become any more embroiled in this situation than she already was? The answer to both those questions was a resounding no! And yet...

'Would it be too much to ask if I could have a cup of coffee while we talk?' Ethan looked up at her gratefully.

The last thing Olivia wanted to do was make him a cup of coffee, and thus delay his departure from her apartment any further. But one glance at the strain so evident beside his eyes and mouth and she relented enough to go out into the kitchen and make them both coffee.

Whatever Ethan and Shelley had had to say to each other this evening, it obviously hadn't resulted in Shelley coming back with him to collect Andrea. Which was a little ominous, to say the least.

'Thanks.' Ethan took the mug of coffee from her as she held it out to him a few minutes later. 'I am sorry about my hurried departure earlier,' he apologised. 'But I had learnt from a mutual friend where I could find Shelley, and I wanted to get there before she realised I was on my way and had a chance to disappear.'

Olivia sat down in the armchair facing his, quietly sipping her own coffee as she waited for him to continue; after all, he was the one who wanted to talk.

Ethan breathed deeply after sipping the reviving coffee. 'This is good coffee,' he said approvingly.

Which made Olivia realise it had been some time since she had made coffee for anyone but herself...

Strange, but in the time she had lived in this apartment she couldn't remember ever inviting anyone back here—not even a female friend. She hadn't known until this moment just how reclusive she had become...

'I'm just delaying things, aren't I?' Ethan acknowledged, completely misunderstanding the reason for Olivia's sudden silence.

'You really don't have to tell me anything,' she assured him softly.

'Oh, but I do,' he asserted firmly. 'I've inadvertently involved you in this tangle; the least I owe you is an explanation. You see—' He broke off as the sound of Andrea's crying from the bedroom suddenly filled the air. 'I think I need to have a word with that young lady about her sense of timing,' he said affectionately, putting his empty coffee mug down on the table before standing up. 'I'll go,' he assured Olivia as she would have stood up too. 'After all, you've stood the evening shift!'

Olivia sank back down into her armchair, watching him as he strode over to her bedroom door and quietly let himself in, speaking soothingly to Andrea as he did so. In truth, after Ethan's innocently spoken words, she couldn't have stood up now if she had wanted to!

She was glad of the respite of his absence; he could have no idea of how his casual comment had evoked painful memories—memories that had been forcing themselves back into her conscious thoughts more and more the last couple of days. No, Ethan could have no idea—and Olivia intended making sure it stayed that way!

Although she couldn't say she was altogether sure

she was happy with his presence in the intimacy of her bedroom—no matter how innocent his reason for being there. It was so obviously a completely feminine room, with its lace and satin décor in creams and golds, and only the presence of a double bed gave evidence that she hadn't always slept alone...

'Is she hungry again, do you think?' Ethan asked concernedly as he returned with the still crying Andrea in his arms.

'She could be,' Olivia agreed, standing up. 'I'll go and warm one of the bottles you left earlier.'

In fact, Olivia had been amazed by his organisation when she'd opened Andrea's bag earlier. There was everything in there, including several made-up bottles of formula, that she could possibly need to look after the baby for several hours.

Curiously, Ethan Sherbourne was proving more and more just how inexperienced he *wasn't* when it came to caring for a young baby...

'This is cosy, isn't it?' Ethan remarked several minutes later, with the baby lying in his arms sucking contentedly on her bottle as he once again sat in the armchair opposite Olivia's.

It wasn't quite the description Olivia would have used; overly familiar was what sprang to *her* mind. In fact, explanation or not, she couldn't wait for Ethan to leave now—and take the baby Andrea with him!

'It's rather late,' she replied tersely, deliberately not answering his own comment. After all, there was no reason why he couldn't go back to his own apartment and feed Andrea there. And leave her in peace.

'You're right; it is.' Ethan grimaced in agreement

after glancing at the clock on her fireplace, which now read fifteen minutes after midnight. 'Young babies have no appreciation of the difference between day and night, do they?' he added with a fond glance at the obviously alert Andrea.

'How should I know?' Olivia returned stiffly.

'You shouldn't,' he accepted lightly. 'By the way,' he added softly, 'Happy Christmas.'

Olivia opened startled grey eyes, before frowning heavily. Of course, they were now fifteen minutes into Christmas Day. She swallowed hard. 'Happy Christmas, Ethan.' Her voice choked on its unfamiliarity with those two words.

He gave her that spontaneous grin once again. 'I bet I'm the last person you thought you'd be saying that to this year!' he said, explaining his humour.

Or any other year! Ethan Sherbourne just wasn't the type of man she wanted to spend any time with—let alone the early hours of Christmas morning.

'I'm sure you could say the same thing about me.'

Ethan gave her a considering look, head tilted on one side, those brown eyes darkly probing. 'Why should you think that?' he finally asked—just when Olivia had almost got to the stage where she thought she couldn't stand that piercing gaze on her a moment longer!

Now it was Olivia's turn to smile. 'I'm hardly the type of woman you would usually choose to spend time with,' she stated derisively.

He frowned his puzzlement. 'And how would you know what type of woman that is?'

Her smiled widened. 'I've seen several of them in

passing, on their way up to your apartment,' she told him candidly.

He looked at her quizzically for several long minutes. 'But don't you know what I do—?' He broke off as Andrea, having let the bottle slip from her mouth, now let out a sound of protest at being deprived her food. 'Silly pumpkin,' Ethan murmured indulgently as he repositioned the bottle.

Olivia stood up abruptly, unable to stand the intimacy of this situation a moment longer. They might almost have been a family. A father and mother talking softly together as the baby was fed. It was an image that was totally unacceptable to her.

'Would you like some more coffee?' she offered abruptly.

'That's very kind of you,' Ethan said warmly. 'But I really think Andrea and I have taken up enough of your time for one evening,' he added with obvious regret.

From the look of the milk still left in the bottle, and the speed with which Olivia knew the baby drank, he was going to be here for some time yet. 'It will only take me a second or so to pour it; it's already made in the percolator,' she assured him, and she picked up his empty mug. Once again she needed a few minutes to herself, and getting fresh coffee provided her excuse to leave the room.

'In that case…thanks.' He made himself more comfortable by sliding down the chair. 'If it's any consolation, Olivia,' he called after her as she went through to the kitchen, 'this isn't quite how I envisaged spending my Christmas, either!'

Which was exactly what Olivia needed to hear to put her equilibrium back on its usual even keel!

Of course this wasn't how Ethan had expected to spend his Christmas! No doubt he had one—or possibly several—of his harem lined up with whom to spend the hours of Christmas. But baby Andrea's appearance had ensured that just wouldn't happen.

And, Olivia told herself firmly before returning to the sitting room, she mustn't ever think Ethan was doing more than playing with her, in the absence of one of those women, with his occasional flirtatious remarks to her. The poor man probably couldn't help himself! To imagine anything else would be pure stupidity on her part.

'Are you doing anything tomorrow—I mean today?' Ethan asked conversationally, after glancing at the clock once again.

Olivia slowly put his coffee mug down on the table in front of him before moving decisively back to her own chair. What business was it of his how she intended spending her Christmas?

She thought longingly of the two new classical CDs she had bought to listen to during the next two days. She had no intention of even switching the television on for any of that period; the superficial, over-jolly seasonal programmes were total anathema to her. She had bought a delicious Dover sole to grill for her lunch today, knowing it would be very enjoyable with a glass of light white wine.

Yes, her Christmas—such as it was—was all taken care of.

'It's Christmas Day,' she answered dismissively.

'Exactly.' Ethan grinned.

'I meant there will be nowhere open,' she said coolly.

'I meant, are you going away to see family? Or anything?' he pursued lightly.

Olivia wasn't fooled for a moment. By 'anything' he was obviously referring obliquely to the possibility that she might have a male friend she was seeing.

She thought briefly of Dennis Carter, who had casually suggested that he might call her on Boxing Day, to wish her a Merry Christmas. Somehow Olivia had the feeling his telephone call might include an invitation to spend the day with him.

'I am spending the holiday period at home. Alone,' she added bravely.

'Come upstairs and spend the day with Andrea and me,' Ethan suggested instantly, sitting forward to look at her intently. 'Don't refuse until you've thought about it, Olivia,' he said as she would have done exactly that.

She didn't need to think about it; the idea of spending Christmas day—any day!—in the company of Ethan Sherbourne, with or without the presence of baby Andrea, was totally unacceptable to her. Although without Andrea the invitation would probably never have been made at all...

'I've been out and bought a tree, and decorations,' Ethan added persuasively. 'In fact, the tree still needs to be trimmed,' he admitted. 'I'm not sure where the time went today—yesterday—but I simply didn't have time to do anything but put the tree in a pot.' He looked around Olivia's apartment, which was totally lacking in any sign that it was indeed Christmas, least of all a decorated tree surrounded by presents! 'We could do it together later this morning, before opening our presents,' he suggested cajolingly.

Olivia had listened with growing horror as he outlined his plans for today—for all of them! 'I—'

'I've bought you a Christmas present, Olivia,' Ethan put in softly. 'At least, Andrea and I have,' he added huskily.

Olivia's stare was now one of shocked amazement, her cheeks fiery red. What did Ethan think he was doing, buying her a Christmas present? He had no right—

She didn't have anything to give him in return! Or Andrea either, for that matter...

'Do come, Olivia,' Ethan persuaded, putting the now replete Andrea into her pushchair before gathering up her things in preparation for leaving. 'It will be much more fun. For Andrea, I mean. And you did say you don't have any other plans...'

It was time to stop this. And stop this now! 'Andrea is hardly old enough to care one way or the other,' Olivia replied sharply.

Ethan looked sad as he straightened. 'But *I* would know, Olivia,' he said. 'This is her first ever Christmas, don't forget. I want it to be special for her.'

Olivia could hardly see how her own presence would make it that! 'I said I was spending Christmas alone,' she bit out harshly. 'And that's because that's the way I prefer to spend it,' she concluded rudely.

Ethan unconcernedly wheeled Andrea's laden pushchair towards the door. 'No one should spend Christmas Day alone,' he said lightly. 'We'll expect you about nine-thirty, okay?'

No, it was not okay! Of all the arrogant—

'Ethan—' Olivia broke off as he stopped suddenly in front of her, bending to pick something up off the floor. 'What on earth is that?' She peered at the piece of green foliage Ethan now held in his hand.

Dark brows rose over quizzical brown eyes. 'Don't you know?' Ethan teased, suddenly standing much too close to her.

Olivia resisted the impulse to step back; she was a mature woman of thirty-two, not a gauche teenager!

She frowned down at the sprig of greenery, the white berries that decorated its branches making it unmistakable. Mistletoe! Now how on earth had that got here? She certainly hadn't brought it. Maybe it had got caught up in her shopping at the supermarket earlier, and dropped to the floor as she'd carried the bags inside? However it had got here, she did not like the determined glint in Ethan's eyes as he held the mistletoe up over the two of them!

'It's bad luck not to kiss under the mistletoe,' Ethan told her gruffly.

Olivia found herself held mesmerised by the warmth in those compelling brown eyes. 'I've never heard that before,' she replied breathlessly.

'That's because I just made it up,' Ethan admitted, before his head lowered and his lips claimed hers.

Olivia felt as if an electric shock had coursed through her body at the first touch of those softly sensual lips against hers, which parted slightly as she gasped in reaction. Then the kiss deepened as Ethan's mouth took firm control of hers.

His arms moved about the slenderness of her waist

and he pulled her against the hard length of his body, his hands trailing down the length of her spine.

Olivia wanted to scream, and shout, to push him away—but more than any of those things she wanted the kiss to go on and on for ever!

Her body felt on fire, her limbs fluid, her only reality Ethan and the erotic exploration of his lips against hers.

He was finally the one to break the kiss, his breathing shallow as he rested his forehead against hers. 'Wow!' he murmured throatily.

Wow, indeed. Olivia could never remember being so aroused by just a kiss. And from Ethan Sherbourne of all people…!

'Nine-thirty in the morning?' he prompted, his arms still firmly about her waist.

She moistened dry lips, hardly daring to breathe. 'Yes.'

'Good.' He nodded his satisfaction as he stepped away from her. 'You don't need to bring anything—just yourself,' he said warmly.

Olivia was still standing where he had left her as he quietly closed the door behind him and Andrea as they left. She didn't dare move yet, in case her legs didn't hold her when she did!

Worst of all, despite her earlier protestations, she now seemed to have agreed to spending Christmas Day with Ethan and his young charge!

'The mistletoe was a nice touch,' Mrs Heavenly praised Faith warmly.

Faith made no response. Arranging for that piece of mistletoe to be there in front of the door, where Ethan would easily find it as he left, had been a brainwave on her part. But she didn't want to sound as if she were feeling too self-satisfied; there was still a long way to go on this assignment.

Although that kiss under the mistletoe *had* resulted in Olivia agreeing to spend Christmas Day with Ethan and the baby...

'This evening alone with Andrea was very hard on Olivia,' Faith said instead. 'Are you sure she's up to spending Christmas Day *en famille*?'

Mrs Heavenly smiled sadly. 'I have a feeling it will either be the making or the breaking of her.'

That was what Faith felt too. 'I'm not sure—'

'Olivia lacks faith in herself, as well as in other people, my dear,' Mrs Heavenly pointed out gently. 'One day, in order to start living again, rather than just existing, she has to make a leap of faith. I believe Ethan Sherbourne has been chosen for her to leap to.'

'Which is where I come in,' Faith put in. 'But I do wish Ethan had had the chance to finish explaining to Olivia about those other women in his life.'

Was it her imagination, or did Mrs Heavenly's cherubic gaze suddenly not quite meet her own? Surely she hadn't—?

No, of course not. She was being silly. This was Faith's assignment. Mrs Heavenly wouldn't have given it to her if she hadn't thought she could handle it.

'All in good time, my dear. All in good time,' Mrs Heavenly dismissed brightly. 'Now, if I were you, while Olivia is sleeping I would take a few earthly hours' rest myself.' She beamed up at Faith. 'This promises to be a very busy day for you.'

It certainly did. Faith only hoped Olivia wouldn't change her mind later that morning, and cancel spending the rest of the day with Ethan and Andrea...

CHAPTER SIX

SHE must have changed her mind about the sensibility of spending the day with Ethan and Andrea at least a hundred times since early that morning! After Ethan had left, during the long sleepless early hours, and again after she'd got up and showered. But, despite all that indecision, it was now nine-thirty and she was standing outside Ethan's apartment, preparing to ring the doorbell in order to announce her presence.

It was all the fault of that piece of mistletoe, of course; Olivia still had no idea where it could possibly have appeared from. But without that Ethan would never have kissed her—and she wouldn't have responded!

She still felt a fluttering sensation in her chest every time she thought of that kiss they had shared. Her only consolation was that it probably hadn't meant a thing to Ethan; he probably viewed kissing her as having done his good deed for the day!

'Merry Christmas!' Ethan greeted as he opened the apartment door and kissed her lightly on the cheek. 'Come in.' He clasped her arm to pull her inside. 'You're just in time to watch Andrea open her presents.'

Olivia stared in astonishment at the tiny baby as she lay on the thickly carpeted floor, surrounded by more Christmas presents than Olivia had ever seen before!

'Do you think I went a bit overboard?' Ethan said uncertainly as he saw her expression. 'This is such a completely novel experience for me,' he explained. 'I almost bought the toy store out!'

She wouldn't be at all surprised. And some of the things he had purchased were obviously way beyond Andrea's age range—the tricycle, for example. But no doubt Andrea would grow into it.

As for the novelty factor; no doubt finding out he was a father *was* a novel experience for him!

'They must have loved you,' she teased, before going down onto the carpet next to Andrea. She was dressed smartly but comfortably today, in black trousers and a red jumper, as Christmas was being foisted on her anyway, she had decided she might as well enter into the Christmas spirit! 'Happy Christmas, poppet.' She kissed Andrea on one creamy brow. 'I brought you a present too.' She held up the gift wrapped in pink tissue paper.

'That's really kind of you,' Ethan said admiringly as he watched her unwrap the present for the baby.

Having Ethan tell her earlier that he had a Christmas present for her had initially put her in rather an awkward position—because she didn't have one for him. Or Andrea. But then she'd thought hard... Ethan hadn't been too difficult to sort out; she had simply wrapped up the two CDs she had originally bought herself for Christmas. Andrea had been a different matter alto-gether...

'Christmas is for children,' she answered Ethan distractedly, holding up the brightly coloured rattle that she had just unwrapped. As with all young babies, Andrea was transfixed.

'You know something,' Ethan said slowly as he watched Andrea excitedly waving her arms as Olivia gently shook the rattle. 'I think I should have saved myself the trouble of buying all this—' he waved his arm over the pile of unwrapped presents '—and just bought her one of those!'

'It's a little like when we were children and found the boxes more interesting than the contents!' Olivia laughed in agreement. 'But don't worry; she'll grow into all of these,' she assured him lightly.

But her mood wasn't in the least light as she waited for his next question, which was sure to be where, exactly, had the rattle come from? Because it obviously wasn't the sort of thing one had just lying around in case a baby came to visit. If Ethan asked, she had decided she was going to tell him that she had been out yesterday and bought the small gift for Andrea...

'This is for you.' She held out the other slender parcel she had brought with her.

He frowned at the present. 'Olivia, you really didn't have to—'

'*I* was always taught to say, "Thank you very much. It's very kind of you",' she rebuked gently.

He looked decidedly uncomfortable. 'Thank you very much. And it *is* very kind of you. I just—'

'You don't know what it is yet,' she interjected, relieved when he at last took the present, and turning away to play with Andrea while he unwrapped it, suddenly feeling embarrassed. What if he didn't like classical music? What if—?

'I can't believe this!' Ethan burst out incredulously seconds later. 'It's amazing. I actually went out yesterday intending to buy myself this particular CD.' He held up the Mozart. 'I just didn't have time after going to the toy shop.'

'You probably wouldn't have been able to carry it, either.' Olivia looked at the pile of presents under the tree still to be opened, slightly incredulous herself that Ethan should have the same taste in music as herself. Incredulous that they should have anything in common at all!

'Probably not.' He chuckled. 'Is it okay with you if I put this on now?'

'It's your gift,' she replied.

'In that case...' He suited his actions to his words, then came back to sit with Olivia and Andrea under the enormous tree, the beautiful sound of Mozart's music filling the apartment. 'This is for you.' He picked up a parcel, the red shiny paper adorned with gold ribbon and a bow. 'I'm useless at wrapping gifts, so I had the woman in the shop wrap it for me,' he admitted.

Olivia's hand shook slightly as she accepted the present. It was light, and soft to the touch, making her wonder what could possibly be inside. She was almost afraid to open it and find out!

'It won't bite.' Ethan grinned at her obvious hesitation, brown eyes warm with humour. 'I told the saleslady that you were probably a 32D, but you can always take it back and change it if I got the size wrong—'

'Ethan!' Olivia gasped her protest—and not just at

his implication that the parcel contained a bra. He had also guessed her bust size exactly!

He laughed. 'Just trying to stay in character for you,' he explained. 'I had the distinct impression last night that you believe me to be something of a womaniser...'

Olivia avoided meeting that humorous brown gaze, deliberately ignoring his last remark as she spoke. 'I don't believe for a moment that there's a bra in here!' she exclaimed.

'A bikini?' he taunted.

'Wrong time of year!'

'A slinky camisole?'

Her cheeks were the bright red of her jumper by this time. 'Not that, either,' she retorted firmly, putting herself out of her agony—and depriving Ethan of his source of teasing!—by ripping open the glossy red paper.

Inside, wrapped in tissue paper, was a delicate cashmere wrap the colour of milky coffee.

Olivia eyes filled with tears as she looked at it and touched its beauty. It was years since anyone had bought her a completely personal gift like this; her usual Christmas presents consisted of products for the bath or chocolates from the far-flung members of her family. Her parents always sent her a cheque, with the excuse that they had 'no idea what to buy her'.

This wrap, exactly the right colour to complement her fair colouring, was so—so absolutely right...

'Do you like it?' Ethan said uncertainly at her continued silence.

'Do I *like* it!' Olivia looked up at him, her eyes still swimming with those unshed tears. 'I love it!' She held the wrap close against her chest.

He looked at her quizzically for several long seconds. 'You know,' he said slowly, 'and please don't take this wrongly!—but I always thought you were rather a cold lady. Distant. Happy keeping yourself to yourself.' He shook his head. 'In the space of the last fifteen minutes I've seen you laugh and I've seen you almost cry. What—or who—have you been hiding from, Olivia?' he prompted.

She swallowed hard, wondering what Ethan would say if she were to answer *herself*...?

The last ten years she had deliberately presented herself with a gruelling schedule. After having worked to put herself through university, and struggled for several years at the bottom of the ladder, very rarely taking time off, she now found herself as junior partner in a prestigious law firm. But it had all been done at a price: no self-questioning...

And she wasn't sure she was up to Ethan questioning her now, either!

'You're being silly,' she dismissed, turning away abruptly, folding the red paper back over the wrap before putting the present to one side and turning back to Andrea. The baby, at least, was still gurgling happily.

There was a continued silence behind her for several minutes, as if Ethan were weighing up the pros and cons of persisting with his questioning...

Olivia held her breath as she waited for his decision.

'We can't just sit here doing nothing, woman,' he finally said briskly. 'There's still a tree to dress, and then vegetables to prepare for Christmas lunch!'

Olivia stood up, moving Andrea to a safer place away from the base of the tree they were going to decorate. 'Are we having turkey for lunch?' She couldn't keep the surprise out of her voice.

'Of course,' Ethan confirmed in a tone that questioned if there was anything else they could possibly have for lunch on Christmas Day. 'I'll have you know I got up at six o'clock this morning to put it in the oven!'

'I'm impressed,' Olivia teased.

'So you should be,' he responded. 'Here, have some tinsel.' He handed her a bright green string of it from the box of decorations.

'The lights should go on first; that way you don't knock the other things off,' she told him knowledgeably.

'I stand corrected,' he returned with a mocking bow, bending down to pick up a box of coloured lights and then handing the plug to her. 'Better?'

'Much,' Olivia answered dryly, turning to watch as he draped the lights over the branches.

It was rather a large tree, reaching almost to the ceiling, and it took them well over an hour to hang all the decorations. But the end result, they both agreed, was well worth the effort.

In fact, as the two of them stood back to admire their handiwork, Olivia thought she had never seen such a beautiful tree. It made her feel like crying all over again!

Strange—in the last forty-eight hours she had cried more than she had allowed herself to do over the last ten years. Oh, she was well aware that Andrea was the prime reason for this breach in her defences, but Ethan had his own way of breaking them down too...

She gave an involuntary start now as she felt his arm drop lightly onto her shoulders, turning to look at him questioningly.

'Now it really is Christmas,' he said.

The room sparkled and danced as the tree decorations reflected the illumination from the coloured lights, the whole thing giving the room a magical air.

'I don't think your youngest guest is too impressed,' Olivia said wryly, giving a pointed look in Andrea's direction, relieved to have something to break the spell of enchantment she had felt stealing over her.

Christmas was like that, she told herself firmly, a time to be over-emotional. It had nothing to do with Ethan. Or with her.

The baby, obviously tired out from her unusual morning, had fallen asleep on the carpeted floor.

Olivia felt an emotional lump in her throat as she watched Ethan gently pick the baby up in his arms before carrying her through to his bedroom.

Over-emotional or not, she realised she couldn't stand much more of this. She felt constantly on the edge of tears. The memories that were crowding in on her becoming almost unbearable.

'What is it, Olivia?'

She turned sharply at the sound of Ethan's voice, realising that her emotions must have been reflected on her face as she saw the way he was looking at her so concernedly.

'Don't!' she choked, giving a desperate shake of her head. His kindness was something she couldn't take at this moment—not when she was already feeling so vulnerable and exposed.

He strode forcefully across the room, grasping the tops of her arms to look down at her searchingly. 'Talk to me, Olivia,' he encouraged huskily. 'Tell me what it is that's tearing you apart in front of my eyes?'

She couldn't! If she once started talking she knew she wouldn't be able to stop. It was something she just didn't dare do.

'Olivia?' He shook her slightly in his frustration at her silence.

She swallowed hard, fighting back her feelings of panic; she didn't have to do anything she didn't want to do! 'I thought you said we had some vegetables to prepare,' she reminded him stiltedly.

'Damn the vegetables!' he barked impatiently. 'I don't know what this is, what happened to you in the past, but you need to talk to someone, Olivia—'

'Aren't you being rather arrogant in assuming that someone should be you?' she cut in, blonde brows raised as she met his gaze unflinchingly, her defences firmly back in place after his attempt to step over a line she allowed no one to cross. Absolutely no one!

Ethan's mouth tightened at her deliberate challenge. 'I don't see any other men lining up for the privilege!' he responded harshly.

Olivia flinched at his own deliberate retaliation. Obviously they were both people who came out fighting if they felt they were being backed up against a wall!

'Your arrogance is in assuming I wish to confide in anyone, let alone you!' she returned hardily, grey eyes glittering with anger now.

Ethan stared down at her wordlessly for several long seconds before releasing a hissing breath. 'I realise it's what you're angling for, but I refuse to fight with you.' He shook his head. 'Today of all days!'

'Peace on earth, goodwill to all men and all that,' Olivia replied derisively.

'And all women,' Ethan drawled, releasing her to step back.

Olivia felt suddenly cold with the removal of his hands from her arms. 'I thought the last applied to you the rest of the year, too,' she said tersely.

His eyes narrowed at the barb. 'Back to the woman-iser accusation, are we?' he countered. 'Things are very rarely what they seem to someone on the outside, Olivia.'

'I don't believe Andrea is a figment of my imagi-nation!' Olivia returned staunchly.

'Andrea?' he repeated. 'What does she have to do with it?'

What—!

'Well, if you don't know, I'm not about to tell you!' Olivia snapped disgustedly.

Was the man totally beyond conscience? Beyond shame? Oh, not for the fact that he wasn't married to Andrea's mother; it seemed that was many men's personal choice nowadays. But nothing could alter the fact that Shelley hadn't trusted him enough to confide her problems to him. Or that he had continued with his own rakish lifestyle long after their affair was over...!

Ethan drew in a harshly controlling breath. 'I realise my efforts as a grandfather may not meet your exacting standards, but I can assure you that I am doing my very best to make this as good a Christmas for Andrea as I possibly can...'

Olivia didn't hear another word he said after 'grandfather'. *Grandfather!* He was Andrea's grandfather—not her father, as Olivia had assumed?

Assumed...

Yes, she had assumed, given all the circumstances, that he had to be the baby's father. But no one—not Shelley, nor Ethan himself—had actually said that he was.

Maybe, in the circumstances, it hadn't been such an unusual assumption to make. But, as it now turned out, it had been an erroneous one.

She couldn't believe it; Ethan was Andrea's *grandfather*!

'I had no idea Ethan was Andrea's grandfather!' Faith exclaimed concernedly, knowing that she had been guilty of making an assumption too.

Mrs Heavenly looked up in surprise. 'Back again already, my dear?' she said kindly.

Faith drew in a deep breath. 'I said—'

'I heard you, my dear,' the elderly angel replied soothingly. 'Would it have made any difference if I had told you all the circumstances behind Andrea's birth? After all, it's Olivia who asked for our help, not Ethan,' she reminded her gently.

Faith shifted uncomfortably, reluctant to admit that until a few moments ago, when Ethan had revealed that he was Andrea's grandfather, and not her father, she had been feeling the same prejudice towards him that Olivia obviously had. Angels weren't supposed to feel prejudice...

'Probably not,' she answered evasively. 'I was just a little—surprised to learn the truth, that's all.'

Mrs Heavenly smiled. 'Not as much as Olivia was, I'm sure!'

'No,' Faith acknowledged ruefully, clearly remembering that stunned look on Olivia's beautiful face. 'Maybe there is hope for those two finding each other, after all…' she added thoughtfully, as she remembered that other emotion on Olivia's face as she'd looked at Ethan with new eyes.

'I told you. It's faith that's needed in this case, my dear,' Mrs Heavenly reiterated.

'Of course,' Faith accepted, knowing herself to be mildly, if kindly, rebuked and straightening determinedly. 'I'll get back and see what I can do to help.'

'You do that, dear,' Mrs Heavenly agreed, blue eyes warm. 'I must say I think it's all going extremely well so far,' she said happily.

'You do?' Faith said hopefully.

'Of course.' Mrs Heavenly smiled. 'Don't you think so?'

'Ethan is really rather a nice man, isn't he?' she realised slowly.

'Nothing less would do for someone as special as Olivia,' Mrs Heavenly assured her.

That was what Faith had thought. Had realised. Now all she had to do was return to Earth and avert the argument that had been brewing when she left.

She only hoped she hadn't left it too late!

CHAPTER SEVEN

Now that she knew the truth, Olivia could view Ethan's behaviour over the last couple of days from a new perspective, and there was respect for him in her eyes now as she looked across the room at him.

Whatever plans of his own he might have had for Christmas, they had obviously been shelved in favour of Andrea's needs. In fact, not only had he put his own life on hold, he had gone out of his way to make this Christmas as wonderful for Andrea as it was possible for him to do so. Olivia very much doubted he usually bothered with a tree—or lunch with all the trimmings, for that matter!

Which begged the question: What sort of man was he really…?

Olivia now found herself unable to answer that question, all her preconceived ideas thrown up in the air.

But how did she begin to get herself out of the situation she had created because of her earlier prejudice…? More to the point, how did she avoid letting Ethan know of her earlier assumption concerning Andrea's paternity! Or did she avoid it at all? Wouldn't it be more honest on her part to own up to her mistake?

It might be more honest, she acknowledged, but she doubted it would be conducive to this being the harmonious Christmas Day Ethan wanted!

'Nothing to say?' he challenged at her continued silence.

Olivia moistened dry lips. 'Ethan, I—' She broke off, drawing in a shaky breath. 'I owe you an apology,' she burst out, before she had a chance to change her mind. 'It was presumptuous of me. I allowed my prejudice towards you to colour my judgement. I had no right to come to such a conclusion.' She was babbling! Worse than that, from the completely puzzled expression on Ethan's face, she was making no sense! 'I'm sorry,' she concluded heavily.

'Glad to hear it,' he accepted lightly. 'Now, would you mind telling me what it is you're sorry for?'

She winced. 'I thought Andrea— You see, Shelley didn't say— *You* didn't say—'

'Just a minute,' Ethan said slowly, frowning now. 'Correct me if I'm wrong, but until my comment a few minutes ago had you been under the misapprehension that I'm Andrea's father?'

Olivia's wince turned to a self-conscious grimace. 'It really was very presumptuous of me—' She broke off as Ethan began to chuckle, staring at him dazedly. 'It isn't funny, Ethan,' she told him crossly. 'I totally misjudged you—'

'Yes, you did,' he acknowledged with a grin. 'But don't you see, Olivia? To your credit, you kept coming back.'

'That was because of Andrea,' she admitted unhappily.

His expression softened at the mention of his grand-daughter. 'She really is lovely, isn't she?'

'She is,' Olivia agreed. 'She's an absolute credit to her mother,' she added.

'I agree,' Ethan said. 'You really thought *I* was the one involved with Shelley?'

Olivia swallowed, knowing from his expression that now he had stopped laughing at her mistake he wasn't at all pleased by her assumption.

'She's only twenty years old, Olivia!' Ethan rasped.

'I realised that,' Olivia admitted. 'I just—I couldn't see any other explanation after she just left Andrea here with you,' she said defensively.

'Hmm,' he snorted. 'Well, as you've probably now realised, I am indeed a father. My son Andrew, who is only twenty-one,' he elaborated pointedly, 'was the one involved with Shelley a year ago.'

Andrea. Andrew. Shelley had named her daughter for the father... Surely that had to mean something?

'Andrew's mother and I were divorced years ago,' Ethan revealed. 'But Andrew and I have continued to have a very close relationship, nonetheless. I only met Shelley once, when he brought her here to dinner.'

He was telling her that that was how Shelley came to know him. And had known where he lived...

Olivia was feeling more and more foolish by the minute!

'And the reason Shelley, out of sheer desperation, brought Andrea here to me was because when she went to Andrew's flat she discovered he was away on a skiing holiday,' Ethan explained evenly.

Olivia's eyes widened. 'Your son lives in London?'

Ethan nodded. 'He's at university here. But don't be under the misapprehension that he's a student starving in a garrett,' he added dryly. 'Andrew lives very comfortably on the allowance I give him!' Too comfortably, his tone seemed to imply.

'You said he's on a skiing holiday?' Olivia prompted softly.

'Not any more,' Ethan assured her. 'I telephoned him early yesterday and told him to get himself back here. To his credit he was absolutely stunned when I told him the reason why. Apparently Shelley hadn't told him of her pregnancy when she broke off their relationship eight months ago.'

'Maybe she didn't know at the time…?' Olivia suggested lamely.

'Oh, she knew,' Ethan replied. 'But she had some misguided idea that she didn't want to force their relationship into something Andrew possibly didn't want just because of her pregnancy. So, instead, she chose to struggle on on her own.' He sighed angrily.

Misguided, perhaps, Olivia acknowledged, but as a woman she could see it from Shelley's point of view. If Andrew had shown no signs of wanting their relationship to be a serious one before the pregnancy, how could she possibly have told him about the baby without feeling she was pressurising him into something he might not want?

Olivia looked serious. 'They're both young…' She could only imagine Andrew's reaction yesterday, on learning he was a father—whether he was pleased or angry at the knowledge. In either case it must have been a shock to be told of Andrea's existence.

'Old enough to have a daughter,' Ethan countered. 'Besides, I was only Andrew's age when he was born.'

'But you've already said your marriage ended in divorce,' Olivia reminded him, determinedly shutting out her own memories of when she was twenty-one.

'Touché,' Ethan allowed. 'But I'm not proposing that the two of them should get married if that isn't what they want. Although I do know that Andrew was very upset when the relationship ended...' he amended thoughtfully.

'That might be a good sign,' Olivia agreed.

'Let's hope so,' Ethan replied. 'I picked Andrew up from the airport last night, and drove him straight to where I knew Shelley was staying. It wasn't exactly an auspicious meeting. Both of them were still too angry—with each other and themselves. But I've suggested that I continue to look after Andrea over Christmas while the two of them sit down and talk to each other. The least they can do is come to some sort of agreement about Andrea's future upbringing that won't result in a repeat of Shelley's recent feelings of desperation. I think that's fair enough, don't you?' He looked at Olivia intently.

What did it matter what she thought? None of this situation was really any of her business. Although that didn't mean she didn't have great admiration for the way Ethan was handling this delicate situation. In fact, she was starting to think he was a pretty wonderful human being!

She nodded abruptly. 'I think that's very fair,' she agreed, her admiration for him deepening by the minute. Not only had Ethan turned his own life upside down in order to look after Andrea, but he was also trying to help her young parents come to some sort of understanding over the situation.

'Good. At last I seem to have done something right in your eyes!'

Olivia stared at him. What could it possibly matter what she thought—of him or this situation…?

'Now, stop diverting my attention, woman,' Ethan said briskly. 'Let's go and prepare those vegetables!'

'You still want me to stay to lunch?' she said, amazed. Considering the strain he had been put under himself the last couple of days, her erroneous assumptions must surely have been the last straw as far as he was concerned?

He looked at her with mocking brown eyes. 'I'll let you know once you've peeled the potatoes,' he teased.

She had been let off lightly, Olivia acknowledged as she followed him through to the kitchen. Ethan had every right to feel absolutely furious with her for her presumptions, but he had chosen to explain the situation to her instead. If the circumstances had been reversed, Olivia knew she wouldn't have been so magnanimous…

Which, to her dismay, only served to prove to her how narrow-minded and self-opinionated she had become these last few years.

She had formed an opinion of Ethan Sherbourne based on…what? Her own assumptions, that was what. Well, she had been completely wrong concerning Andrea, so wasn't it feasible that she was probably wrong in most of her other ideas concerning Ethan, too?

Most of…?

There she went again, qualifying the positive with an added negative. Why couldn't she just admit she had been wrong about Ethan, full stop? He—

'Stop beating yourself up, Olivia.' Ethan cut into her self-disgusted thoughts. 'If it's any consolation, I probably am most of the things you previously thought me.'

She sighed heavily. 'I somehow doubt that very much!'

'That bad, hmm?' He leaned back against one of the kitchen units to look at her assessingly.

'I'm afraid so,' she admitted self-disgustedly.

'Then that makes your being here all the more credible,' he told her warmly. 'Now, peel these potatoes.' He thrust the bag in front of her. 'I shall deal with the carrots and sprouts!' He turned back to take the other vegetables out of the fridge.

She swallowed hard. 'Don't you want to know what I thought?'

'I think I can guess most of it,' he said wryly.

Olivia couldn't even see the potatoes for the first few seconds she was peeling them, her eyes once again swimming with unshed tears.

She really was going to have to stop this, she decided firmly a few minutes later. Either she would have to sit down and have a really good cry, or she would have to get her emotions back under control. It was just that the latter was proving so hard at the moment!

'Olivia…?'

She turned slowly to look up at Ethan. He no longer made any pretence of working beside her, but stood looking at her instead. If, now having had time to think it through, he no longer wanted her to stay and spend Christmas Day with himself and Andrea, she would quite understand. After all—

Her self-berating thoughts came to an abrupt end as Ethan took her firmly in his arms and kissed her soundly on the lips!

An emotional sob caught in her throat as her arms moved convulsively over his shoulders, her lips parting as she began to kiss him back.

How long that kiss lasted Olivia had no idea. Her senses were reeling, every particle of her feeling totally alive.

Ethan pulled back slightly, looking down at her, his eyes dark and unfathomable. 'You are an extremely beautiful woman, Olivia,' he told her gruffly.

She gave a choked laugh, shaking her head. 'I'm narrow-minded. And opinionated. And—' She stopped speaking as Ethan put light fingertips against her lips.

Ethan shook his head. 'You're beautiful. Desirable. Intelligent. Warm. Caring—yes, you are, Olivia,' he insisted as she would have protested. 'Someone, or something, has hurt you very badly. But you can't hide your gentleness when you're with Andrea.'

'She's just a defenceless baby,' Olivia explained, still very aware of the hard strength of his body moulded against hers.

Ethan grinned. 'One you were obviously determined to defend from my inadequacies at baby-minding!'

'How was I to know you had done all this before?' Her voice rose indignantly.

Ethan looked rueful. 'Actually, I haven't—the fact that I didn't play enough of a role in Andrew's babyhood was one of the reasons my wife left me!' he admitted.

Olivia looked up at him quizzically. 'How long were you married?'

'Two years,' he acknowledged reluctantly.

'Two years!' she gasped incredulously.

He shrugged. 'Apparently I wasn't very good at it.'

'But even so—'

'How long were *you* married, Olivia?' Ethan interrupted, his gaze compelling now, his arms tightening about her waist as she would have pulled away.

She glared up at him as she found herself suddenly trapped in his arms. 'Let me go, Ethan!' she erupted.

'Not until you answer me.'

Her eyes became icy as they met his, her body rigid within the confines of his arms. 'What makes you think I've been married?' she scorned.

'This.' He clasped her left hand and raised it into view, his thumb moving lightly over the third finger. 'Strange, isn't it, how the indentation from wearing a ring very rarely goes away, even when the ring is no longer being worn…?'

Olivia looked down at that hand too, easily able to see the indentation he referred to.

She snatched her hand back, pulling sharply out of his arms, breathing raggedly as she stepped away from him, her cheeks pale. 'I did slightly better than you, Ethan.' She spat the words out. 'My marriage lasted just over three years.' To her dismay—and her anger!—her voice broke over those last words. 'But at least I don't fill my life with a load of empty-headed male bimbos in order to make myself feel attractive and wanted!' She was breathing heavily in her agitation, glaring at him defiantly.

Ethan looked at her wordlessly for several long seconds, and then he drew in a harshly controlling breath. 'Peel the potatoes, Olivia,' he rasped.

Her eyes widened. 'I—'

'Before you say something you are definitely going to regret!' he concluded warningly, eyes narrowed to steely slits.

She had already said several things she deeply regretted! But Ethan had touched on a subject that, although almost ten years old, was still raw and painful.

But was that really a valid excuse for the insulting things she had just said to him...?

She shook her head. 'I really think I should leave,' she said flatly.

'For speaking your mind?' Ethan's brows rose, his expression surprised. 'God, Olivia, you don't know how refreshing it is to be with a woman who does exactly that!'

She looked at him. 'You really want me to stay?'

He nodded wordlessly.

Olivia looked puzzled now. 'But why?'

'Someone has to help me eat this huge turkey!' he returned teasingly, before turning back to the task of peeling the carrots.

Olivia could only stare at the broadness of his back, once again left reeling from his unexpected reaction to something she had said or done deliberately to insult and so ultimately antagonise him.

Deliberately because it was a form of defence that had always worked for her in the past. And yet Ethan refused to be offended...

He also kissed her whenever he felt like it. Deep, compelling kisses that made her knees shake and the rest of her body turn to jelly. Worse than that, despite the things she had said to him, she actually liked him. Perhaps more than liked him, she realised with increasing dismay...!

She had to get out of here before she fell completely under his spell!

'It's up to you, of course, to see that she doesn't leave,' Mrs Heavenly told Faith as she appeared beside her.

'I'm working on it,' Faith said, absolutely stunned at the older angel's appearance. Mrs Heavenly knew— She always— 'What are you doing down here?' Faith gasped her shock.

'I just love it here on Earth this time of year.' Mrs Heavenly looked across at the Christmas tree Olivia and Ethan had decorated so companionably earlier that morning, her cherubic features beaming with pleasure. 'It's a beautiful tree, isn't it?' she said happily.

'Yes, but— Mrs Heavenly, Olivia seems—special to you somehow, so if you would like to take over this assignment yourself, I really wouldn't mind,' Faith told her carefully.

'Don't be silly, my dear.' Mrs Heavenly gave another of her cherubic smiles. 'You're doing absolutely marvelously without any help from me.'

Which in no way answered the question of why Mrs Heavenly was taking such a personal interest in Olivia Hardy's future...

'I'll leave you to it, then, Faith,' Mrs Heavenly said.

For how long? Faith wondered as the image beside her shimmered and then disappeared...

CHAPTER EIGHT

'ETHAN, I really think—' Olivia broke off her excuse to leave as the doorbell rang out shrilly.

'Who on earth can that be?' Ethan exclaimed as he put down the knife he had been using and turned to go and answer the door.

Olivia's response was much more marked. It didn't matter who the caller was; it had to be someone who knew Ethan well enough to feel comfortable calling on him on Christmas Day—in which case she would very definitely be in the way!

She followed Ethan reluctantly from the kitchen, hanging back slightly as he moved to open the door.

'Dad...' A tall, dark-haired young man stepped forward to give Ethan a hug.

Andrew, she realised immediately. And standing beside him, looking extremely shy, was Shelley!

Olivia was very definitely in the way!

'Andrew!' Ethan stepped back at arm's length to look at his son. The similarity between the two men was obvious, despite the twenty-year difference in their ages. Both were tall, dark haired, and dark-eyed, though Andrew's looks were still boyishly handsome where his father's had honed down to carved teak.

'What are the two of you doing here?' Ethan asked quizzically.

'Neither of us could stay away from Andrea any longer.' Shelley was the one to answer, her eyes anxious as she looked past Ethan into the apartment, obviously searching for her baby.

Ethan stepped back. 'She's fast asleep in the bedroom on the left,' he told the young mother warmly. 'Go with her, Andrew,' he instructed his son huskily as Shelley hurried past him.

Olivia hung back in the kitchen doorway as she watched the young couple go into the bedroom together, Andrew's expression one of excitement mixed with awe. And no wonder; he was about to see his daughter for the first time!

She turned back to Ethan, able to see the expressions that flitted across his own face as he watched his son about to face fatherhood: love, pride, and lastly regret, for the fact that Andrew was no longer a child himself.

Olivia felt even more of an intruder as she so easily gauged those emotions.

She swallowed hard. 'Ethan…'

He instantly turned to smile at her, at the same time seeming to shake off those feelings of regret. 'It looks as if there might be four of us for lunch,' he said as he strode towards her.

Her eyes widened. 'You can't still want me to stay…?'

'Why can't I?' Ethan queried, bending to kiss her lightly on the lips as he passed her on his way into the kitchen. 'If things have gone as well as I hope they have between Andrew and Shelley then we can all have ourselves a real old-fashioned Christmas!' he added with satisfaction. 'You know—grandparents, parents and grandchild.'

It didn't take too many guesses to realise under which category he thought she came! 'Ethan, for one thing I'm not old enough to be a grandparent,' she began with embarrassment. 'For a second—' She broke off as Ethan swung round and took her in his arms. 'What—?'

'Exactly how old are you?' Ethan demanded to know, easily moulding her body against his.

She frowned up at him, totally stunned at finding herself in his arms yet again. 'Thirty-two. But—'

'Old enough to be the *partner* of a grandparent,' he assured her.

Olivia's eyes widened. 'But I'm not—'

'Dad, is it okay with you if—? Oh!' Andrew stopped abruptly in the doorway as he saw his father wasn't alone, and his euphoric expression turned to puzzled curiosity as he looked at Olivia.

Not just because Ethan wasn't alone, Olivia inwardly panicked, but because he was holding an unknown woman in his arms—unknown to Andrew that was!—in an obviously intimate way!

'It's okay, Andrew,' Ethan said as he turned to face his son, releasing Olivia but still keeping his arm draped across her shoulders. 'You were saying...?' he prompted.

Olivia had never felt so embarrassed in her life, knowing from Andrew's speculative expression as he looked at the two of them that he was drawing his own conclusions concerning their relationship—and coming up with completely the wrong answer!

Andrew gave his father a knowing grin. 'Shelley and I were wondering if it was okay for us to spend the day here with you.' His grin turned to an uncertain frown. 'But obviously that was before I realised—'

'Of course you can all spend the day here.' Ethan cut briskly across his son's awkward glances in Olivia's direction. 'This is Olivia Hardy.' He smiled down at her warmly. 'A special friend of mine,' he added for his son's benefit.

'Olivia,' Andrew greeted.

'Andrew,' she returned, still reeling from Ethan's 'special friend of mine' claim.

'Have you and Shelley managed to sort anything out in the last twelve hours?' Ethan prompted sharply. Obviously the politeness of the introductions was over as far as he was concerned. 'Besides the fact that you both love Andrea, that is,' he added dryly.

That slightly dazed expression returned to Andrew's youthfully handsome face. 'I still can't believed she's real,' he breathed.

'You will once you've done your share of walking up and down with her when she starts teething!' Ethan assured his son.

'I loved Shelley before, and totally disintegrated when she broke off our relationship, but this—! I've asked Shelley to marry me.'

'And?' Only the tightening of Ethan's hand on Olivia's shoulder betrayed his own tension.

Andrew went on, 'She's agreed to a six-month trial

period. Just in case I want to change my mind. Which I won't,' he added firmly. 'I never wanted to break up in the first place, and now that I know the reason for it—! Be prepared for a wedding in six months' time!'

Looking at Andrew Sherbourne was like looking at Ethan as he must have been twenty years ago, Olivia realised. The younger man obviously had the same confidence and determination as his father, although, as far as she could see, Andrew had yet to develop his father's arrogance...

'Unless you were thinking of having one yourself before then...?' Andrew probed, thrusting his hands into the pockets of his denims as he looked speculatively at his father and Olivia.

Ethan looked down at Olivia as he felt her stiffen against him, his brown gaze openly laughing at the panic he easily read in her expression. 'I'll let you know if I do,' he answered his son evenly, those brown eyes continuing to laugh at Olivia's obvious discomfort.

'But don't hold your breath!' Olivia put in sharply, moving slightly so that she was no longer in the curve of Ethan's arm, able to breathe more easily, think more easily, now that she was no longer held against his warm masculinity. 'Now, if you'll all excuse me, I think it's time I went home and—'

'No way,' Ethan said firmly as he guessed what she was about to do. 'Andrew and Shelley have you to thank as much as me for looking after Andrea these last two days. We're all going to spend the day here together, Olivia,' he stated decisively, daring her to continue with her excuses to leave.

The prospect of spending the day with Ethan had been nerve-racking enough, but Olivia could imagine nothing more awful than having to be with his son, son's girlfriend, and baby granddaughter too. Almost, as Ethan had already pointed out, as if they were a family!

'Oh, please don't leave, Olivia!' Shelley had come out of the bedroom, baby Andrea nestled contentedly in her arms. 'For one thing I haven't had a chance to apologise to you for my rudeness the other evening,' she said. 'You must have thought I was awful, just leaving Andrea here in the way that I did—'

'Not at all,' Olivia instantly assured her warmly. 'Motherhood can be—overwhelming, can't it?' she sympathised.

'Yes,' Shelley acknowledged, glancing down at her baby daughter. 'But I've realised this last couple of days just how rewarding it can be too.'

Olivia swallowed hard as she saw the unconditional love in Shelley's face as she looked at her daughter, the emotional lump stuck in her throat preventing her from answering this last remark.

She was never going to get through an afternoon and evening of this!

She drew in a sharp breath. 'I really do have to go back to my own apartment for a few minutes, Ethan,' she told him firmly, not quite meeting his eyes, already knowing the censure she would see there.

'Would the two of you excuse us a few minutes?' Ethan spoke to Andrew and Shelley, but Olivia knew his gaze remained fixed on her.

'Please don't leave on our account, Olivia,' Andrew

told her, before going into the sitting room with Shelley and their daughter, closing the door behind them.

Olivia kept her attention fixed on the third button down on Ethan's shirt. 'Perhaps you could take the opportunity of my absence to explain the real situation to Andrew and Shelley?'

'And what "real situation" would that be, Olivia?' he prompted.

She looked up at him now, blinking as she found herself caught in a feeling of dark warmth. 'That I'm just a neighbour, of course,' she said sharply.

'But you aren't,' Ethan told her softly.

Olivia stared at him searchingly, deciding that she really didn't want to know what he thought she was to him.

'Not to me,' Ethan continued. 'Any more than I believe that's all I am to you, either.'

The experience of caring for a very young baby had certainly broken down the barriers between them in a way that might otherwise have taken months to do—if ever. But that didn't mean Olivia wanted this situation to continue.

She stepped away from him, tilting up her chin challengingly as she looked at him. 'Ethan, I do believe you're allowing the Christmas spirit to affect your judgement,' she told him with deliberate mockery.

He looked totally unconcerned by her obvious sarcasm. 'I haven't had any Christmas spirit yet—but I intend to rectify that by opening a bottle of champagne as soon as you get back!' he said with satisfaction.

In other words, if she wasn't back within a reasonable amount of time he was going to come looking for her!

Damn.

'I'll try not to be too long,' she answered non-committally. After all, she could always barricade herself in—she doubted even Ethan would go to the extreme of battering down her door in order to force her into spending the rest of the day with him!

'Five minutes,' he warned gently as she walked over to the door. 'After that I come looking for you.'

Olivia turned to give him a glare. 'I thought this was still a country with freedom of choice...'

'It is,' Ethan replied unconcernedly.

'As long as my choice fits in with yours!' she guessed.

He grinned across at her. 'You're learning.'

'Ethan, I have no intention of learning anything more about you than I already know. You—'

'Olivia—whoever he is, he isn't good enough to breathe the same air as you,' Ethan cut across her.

'*Who* isn't?'

'The married lover you hope has telephoned and left a message on your answer-machine?' he suggested.

'Married—!' She stared at him incredulously. 'What married lover?' she demanded; where on earth had he come up with this one? The only person who might possibly have left a message on her answer-machine while she was out this morning was Dennis Carter, and he was neither married nor her lover!

Ethan looked at her consideringly, folding his arms across the broadness of his chest. 'I've always wondered about you, Olivia—about the way you live alone, with very few friends visiting and no male visitors at all. But the more I've thought about it the last few days the more I've realised that it's the classic behaviour of a woman involved with a married man.'

Olivia was dumbstruck. Not just by his conclusion—wrong though it was!—but by the fact that Ethan had bothered to think about her in this way at all. She certainly hadn't given *his* private life the same consideration! Probably because his private life read like an open book. At least…she had thought it did…

This was incredible. She had lived her life quietly—reclusively, perhaps—these last ten years, not bothering anyone and not bothered by anyone, either, and yet still it seemed that people made conjectures, drew conclusions…that *Ethan* had drawn one particular conclusion.

'Statistics have proved that those sort of men very rarely leave their wife for the mistress,' Ethan continued gently.

She looked at him in shock. All this time he had thought—believed—! 'Maybe in this case you have that the wrong way round, Ethan—maybe it's me who doesn't *want* him to leave his wife,' she gritted—whoever 'he' might be!

'Like I said, whoever he is, he isn't fit to breathe the same air as you,' Ethan said.

Olivia gave him a pitying glance. 'I'll keep your advice in mind,' she told him tautly. 'Now, if you wouldn't mind, I think I'll just go and check for any messages on my answer-machine!'

'You have five minutes,' he reminded her.

Olivia was so angry as she left that it took every

effort on her part to return Shelley and Andrew's smiles as she walked through the sitting-room to let herself out of the apartment.

She felt stunned as she stepped into the lift, hardly aware of its descent, of walking down the corridor to her own apartment, of letting herself inside.

But as she looked around the cool sterility of her own home—the home that usually offered her peace as well as sanctuary—comparing it with the warmth of Christmas that Ethan had so easily created in the apartment above, she felt a heaviness descend upon her, and dropped down into one of the armchairs to bury her face in her hands.

All this time Ethan had thought—

All the time he had been so kind to her, had kissed her, he had believed—

The life he had described for her—the fact that she lived alone, that few friends visited her, that no men came to her apartment at all—it all seemed so cold and empty after the warmth and laughter she had known with Ethan these last few hours. After the *kisses* she had shared with Ethan these last two days…!

Her face was still white with shock as she straightened, staring sightlessly ahead with huge grey eyes. She hadn't just enjoyed Ethan's company and kisses these last few days—she had fallen in love with him!

Yes, thought Faith as she saw the stunned disbelief of realisation on Olivia's face. Yes, yes, *yes!*

She looked around her for Mrs Heavenly, eager to share her euphoria with her, sure her mentor wouldn't want to miss Olivia's emotional awakening. But for once Mrs Heavenly hadn't appeared to offer her encouragement. Or congratulations.

Faith frowned as Olivia stood up like an automaton, moving woodenly into the bedroom, pulling open the bottom drawer of her bedside cabinet, taking out the photograph that lay there. The tears started to fall as Olivia held the photograph tenderly against her.

Then Faith knew exactly why Mrs Heavenly wasn't here to congratulate her on a job well done. Because this assignment was still far from over...!

CHAPTER NINE

'THE innocence of youth, hmm?' Ethan bent down to whisper in Olivia's ear as she sat in one of the armchairs.

She glanced across the room to where Andrew sat, his arm about Shelley's shoulders as she cuddled Andrea in her arms; they were all fast asleep.

'I thought a post-lunch nap was allowed on Christmas Day,' she said quietly, so as not to disturb the three.

Lunch had been extremely successful; the turkey had been cooked to perfection, as had the vegetables that accompanied it, and afterwards Ethan had brought a flaming, brandy-covered pudding to the table.

'For the oldsters, not the youngsters!' Ethan chuckled ruefully. 'Still, I suppose it *has* been rather an emotional time for them all,' he added with an affectionate smile for his son and his new family.

Olivia had been extremely reluctant to return to Ethan's after the revelation that had hit her earlier in her own apartment, but at the same time had known that if she didn't Ethan would do exactly what he had said he would, and come down to get her.

So she had returned, and to her surprise it had been a very enjoyable lunch, with baby Andrea's presence helping to make it the happy family day that it should be. But now Olivia felt it was time for her to return to her own flat.

'Do you think they'll make it?' Ethan was looking across at the young couple as he moved to sit on the arm of Olivia's chair.

She instantly felt herself tensing at his close proximity, a sudden tightness in her chest making it difficult to breathe too.

This was awful! For ten years she hadn't even looked at a man in a romantic way; how could she possibly have fallen in love with Ethan in only forty-eight hours?

Christmas was a time of miracles…

Now, where on earth had that thought come from? she wondered dazedly. Christmas might be a time of miracles, but what happened once Christmas was over and she was left with an ache inside her that would be her unrequited love for Ethan?

'Olivia…?'

She forced herself to look up at Ethan as she realised he was still waiting for an answer to his question. 'Why shouldn't they make it?' she replied. 'They stand as much chance as any other young couple embarking on a life together. More, probably, because they have Andrea, too,' she added wistfully.

Ethan looked down at her. 'Have you never wanted children of your own, Olivia?'

That tightness in her chest constricted painfully as she stared up at Ethan in disbelief that he could be saying these things to her.

Ethan reached out to cup her chin, his hand gentle, his thumb lightly caressing as he gazed down at her. 'You're so good with Andrea, Olivia. There's no doubt you would make a wonderful mother yourself.'

She drew in a harsh breath, knowing she had to put an end to this conversation—or she was in danger of breaking down again. She had already cried enough for one day.

'Are we back to the subject of my going-nowhere affair with a married man?' she taunted.

Ethan didn't move, but his face took on a hardness that hadn't previously been there. 'Did he telephone and leave you a message?'

There had been two messages on her answer-machine earlier: one from her parents, wishing her Happy Christmas before they went off to spend the day with friends, and a second from Dennis Carter, sorry that he had missed her but assuring her that he would call back later. Which was enough to make her want to leave the answering-machine on for the whole of the holiday!

She coolly returned Ethan's gaze. 'For a relative stranger, you're taking an extraordinary interest in my private life, Ethan,' she derided.

His fingers tightened against her chin. 'We aren't strangers, Olivia.' He spoke gently. 'We never will be again. You—'

'I really don't think this is the time or the place for such a conversation, Ethan.' She glanced pointedly across the room to the sleeping couple and their baby before moving sharply away from him and standing up. 'I've had a lovely time, Ethan, but now—'

'We're way past the polite niceties stage, too,' he

stated determinedly. 'And if you don't think this is "the time or place" for this conversation...' He stood up, crossing the room to take a tight grip of one of her wrists. 'We'll go down to your apartment and finish it,' he told her, pulling her along behind him as he marched forcefully towards the door.

'Ethan, stop this!' she hissed, desperately trying to free her wrist.

'Stop that, or you'll hurt yourself,' was Ethan's grim response to her struggles.

'*I'll—!* Ethan!' she bit out angrily, pulling even harder to free herself.

'Shh.' He turned briefly to silence her. 'You'll wake the children,' he said sardonically, before continuing on his way out of his apartment, pulling Olivia down the corridor and into the lift with him before pressing the button for the floor below.

'But—' Her protest was cut short as Ethan's lips came down forcefully on hers.

Her struggles ceased immediately, with a low groan of surrender in her throat as she gave herself up to the pleasure of that kiss. Her arms were released and she entwined them about Ethan's neck, her body pressed warmly against his.

Ethan was breathing hard by the time he raised his head as the lift came to a halt. 'I'm not going to allow you to retreat back behind those steel bars, Olivia,' he told her fiercely, his hands tightly gripping her upper arms as he stared down at her intently. 'Do you understand me?' He shook her slightly.

She moistened suddenly dry lips before answering him. 'I understand you, Ethan.'

It would be a useless thing to try anyway; loving Ethan in the way she did meant that she had nowhere to hide!

Once again her apartment seemed cold and uninviting in comparison with the warmth she had so recently known in Ethan's home. Would it always feel this way to her now, simply because Ethan wasn't in it? Oh, she hoped not!

She swallowed hard, not knowing what to say now they were completely alone. It might have been hard for her to be in the company of the young couple and their baby most of the day, but being alone here with Ethan was even more uncomfortable!

'I'm in love with you, Olivia.'

She became very still as she stared across the room at him, her blood feeling as if it had turned to ice in her veins. He couldn't really have just said—

'I said I'm in love with you, Olivia,' he repeated harshly.

He *had* said it! But why? What possible reason could Ethan have for saying something like that?

She swallowed again. 'Don't you think you're taking this idea of saving me from myself a little too far?' Did that strange-sounding voice really belong to her?

'Damn saving you from yourself,' Ethan rasped scathingly. 'I want to save you *for me*!' He moved restlessly about the room. 'This last couple of days have been—wonderful. So much so—'

'Wonderful?' Olivia echoed, staring at him incredulously. 'Ethan, you've had baby Andrea left on your doorstep, discovered that you're a grandfather, had your life turned upside down by having to care for her—'

'Andrea was a surprise, yes,' he agreed. 'But she isn't the one who's turned my life upside down,' he assured her, his eyes a warm chocolate-brown as he looked pointedly at her.

Olivia felt the ice melting under the warmth of that gaze, shaking her head to dispel the heat that seemed to be spreading through her body. 'Ethan, what I'm trying to say is that you're disorientated by all that's happened to you the last few days. You've been— forced to distance yourself from—from your normal way of life.' She couldn't quite meet his eyes now, hating even having to mention those other women she knew were in his life.

'Let me get this straight,' he said slowly, looking at her through narrowed lids. 'You think that because I've been unable to see any of my empty-headed bimbos— I think you once called them that?—I've somehow misjudged what's been happening between us?'

'Nothing has been happening between us, Ethan,' Olivia said evasively. 'You—'

'Is that what you think, Olivia?' Ethan persisted.

'Yes!' she answered forcefully.

He began to smile. 'But even *I'm* allowed time off from work over Christmas.'

'Time off from work…?' she repeated. 'But—' She broke off as the telephone began to ring, her heart immediately sinking as she thought she knew who the caller might be. This was definitely not the time for Dennis to call her back!

'Aren't you going to get that?' Ethan prompted as Olivia could only stare across at the telephone in fascinated horror.

'No! I— Yes!' She realised that perhaps she had better, or else Dennis would simply wait for the answer-machine to take over and leave her another message. One that Ethan would hear. Not a good idea, in the circumstances!

'I'll get it,' Ethan told her sharply, calmly picking up the receiver before Olivia could get to it. 'Yes?' he responded coldly. 'No, she isn't. No, she can't come to the phone,' he added hardily. 'Yes, I'll tell her.' He ended the call as abruptly as he had begun it. 'Dennis says to tell you hello, and that he'll see you after Christmas,' he told Olivia, arms folded challengingly across his chest now, as he looked at her.

She shook her head exasperatedly. 'Dennis is a work colleague—'

'I had a feeling he might be,' Ethan replied.

'And just what do you meant by that?' Olivia bridled.

'It's usually the way it works, isn't it?' he said wearily. 'Conversations about how his wife doesn't understand him, how his children all take him for granted, how even the cat ignores him—'

'You're being totally ridiculous now,' she cut in disgustedly. 'For your information Dennis doesn't have a wife, children—or a cat!'

Ethan looked at her with steely eyes. 'Then why isn't he here with you?'

'Because I don't want him to be!' she said agitatedly. 'Because he *is* just a work colleague! To me, at least,' she concluded awkwardly as she remembered Dennis's fumbled kiss at the party.

'Ah!' Ethan pounced knowingly.

'Make your mind up, Ethan.' She sighed her frustration. 'Either Dennis is or is not this married man I'm supposedly having an affair with!'

'It appears that…he isn't,' Ethan admitted. 'That perhaps he isn't the answer at all,' he continued consideringly.

'Back to the drawing board, hmm?' Olivia scorned.

'I'm not going back to anything, as far as you're concerned, Olivia,' he assured her firmly. 'I've told you I'm in love with you.'

'You don't even know me!' she replied exasperatedly.

'As well as you know me,' he returned sardonically.

'Which isn't very well!' she insisted.

'No?' Even as he spoke he took a step towards her, his arms slowly encircling her waist as he gently pulled her against him, her body fitting perfectly to his. 'I know you, Olivia,' he told her. 'And you definitely know me, too,' he added, as her breasts hardened against his chest.

'You're talking about physical compatibility,' she told him desperately, very much afraid that no matter what she might say her body was betraying her instinctive response to him.

She had never known anything like this before. She had loved Simon, spent some wonderful years with him, and yet she could never remember feeling this breathless need for him, this complete awareness of another human being, this physical ache for possession that she knew every time Ethan touched her…!

Ethan went on, 'I'm talking about love, Olivia. The burning need to be with a certain person, the ache to love and protect her for the rest of your lives. The wanting to make her your wife.'

Her gasp was one of surprise. 'You told me you've already tried being married, that you weren't any good at it,' she reminded him breathlessly.

'I was twenty-one years old. What the hell did I know then of lifelong love, let alone the commitment of marriage?' he said self-disgustedly.

Olivia looked up at him, tears swimming in her eyes. 'But you think you know about those things now?'

His mouth tightened as he heard the mockery in her voice. 'I don't think it at all—I know it.'

She shook her head, blinking back the tears. 'There's some things about me that you need to know before you go any further with this conversation.'

His arms remained like steel bands about her waist as he refused to let her go. 'Olivia, nothing you can say is going to change the way I feel about you.'

She wanted so badly to melt in his arms, to say yes to whatever he wanted from her, to never have to be without this man ever again. But she had so much emotional baggage, so many things that Ethan just didn't know...

'Let me go, Ethan,' she told him strongly, easily releasing herself as he relaxed his hold, stepping back determinedly. 'I—'

'I don't remember seeing this here last night...' Ethan bent to pick something up from the coffee table.

Olivia paled as Ethan straightened and she saw the photograph he now held in his hands. How had that got there? She had looked at the photograph earlier, just to remind herself before she went back up to Ethan's apartment. She didn't remember leaving it here when she left...

But she must have done. How else could it have got from her bedroom to the sitting-room...?

How else, indeed? Faith wondered, frowning.

'I put it there.'

Faith turned slowly to Mrs Heavenly, no longer surprised at the way the elderly angel kept appearing like this. But she *was* surprised at what Mrs Heavenly had just said concerning the photograph...

'I don't understand,' Faith responded.

That wasn't exactly accurate. She understood completely what Mrs Heavenly had just said to her; what she didn't understand was the way Mrs Heavenly had taken things into her own hands. Didn't she think Faith was capable—?

'You're more than capable, my dear,' Mrs Heavenly assured her as she easily read Faith's troubled thoughts, her blue gaze very direct as she looked at Faith. 'I just...' She sighed. 'I shouldn't have interfered, I know that. It's just that—I was unsuccessful in helping Olivia ten years ago,' she added heavily. 'I would hate us not to succeed a second time simply because of Olivia's lack of faith in herself.'

'You—?' Faith gasped, glancing at the troubled Olivia before turning back, wide-eyed, to Mrs Heavenly. 'But I thought this was the first time Olivia had sent up a prayer like this...' It was the impression Mrs Heavenly had given her, at least...

The elder angel smiled shyly. 'I wasn't always in the position you see me in now, my dear. Ten years ago I

was the angel assigned to help Olivia in her despair,'
Mrs Heavenly told her sadly. 'I failed her—failed to
convince her that there is a time and a purpose for everything. Her prayer for help two days ago answered
one of my own prayers, too,' she confided. 'One that
I've had for so long *I* was the one who was beginning
to despair. I only hope that at long last they're both
going to be answered.' Her gaze was intense as she
turned back to look at Olivia.

Faith stared at her mentor. Somehow she had never
imagined Mrs Heavenly as being in the same position
as herself. Or that Mrs Heavenly could ever have failed
in one of her own assignments...

But if Mrs Heavenly had failed ten years ago, Faith
wondered, what chance had she of succeeding now—
even with Mrs Heavenly's help...?

CHAPTER TEN

OLIVIA watched Ethan frown darkly as he looked down at the photograph he held, knowing exactly what he would see there, no longer needing to look at it herself. The image was burnt inside her head, to be conjured up whenever she needed it.

He would see a young man, boyishly handsome, with a six-month-old baby held securely in his arms, both of them laughing at the camera. Both of them laughing at *Olivia* as she took the photograph...

'My husband Simon and my son Jonathan.' Olivia spoke woodenly, her eyes deep grey orbs in the paleness of her face.

Ethan didn't move, simply raised his gaze to look at her searchingly. 'What happened to them?'

'They died,' she said harshly, forcing herself to meet his searching gaze. 'Ten years ago. In a road accident. I—I survived.' She spat the last detail out fiercely.

Ethan put the photograph down to give her a considering look. 'Did you?' he finally asked gently.

She drew in a sharp breath. 'Of course I—'

'Somehow I don't think so, Olivia.' Ethan slowly

shook his head, his dark gaze unfathomable as he continued to look at her. 'Oh, physically you may have survived,' he conceded. 'But, unless I'm mistaken, you let the spirit that is Olivia Hardy die along with them.'

She had heard all this before. *Life has to go on, Olivia. You mustn't bury yourself along with them, Olivia. You're still young enough to find love again, Olivia.* And finally, exasperatedly, *We can't help you if you aren't willing to help yourself, Olivia.* Oh yes, she had heard it all before—it was the reason she was now estranged from her own parents.

They meant well; she knew that. Knew that they loved her too, that it had hurt them deeply when she'd begun to distance herself from them all those years ago, until their relationship became the strained one it now was. But she just couldn't bear to hear those things from them any more—knew that nothing anyone could say to her could ever bring back the two people she had loved so dearly.

Except…against all the odds…she was now in love with Ethan Sherbourne!

She looked at him now, a shutter down over the emotions in her eyes. 'I can't love anyone ever again, Ethan,' she told him bleakly.

'Can't?' he repeated. 'Or won't?'

She flinched at the challenge in his voice. 'What difference does it make which it is?' She turned away. 'The conclusion is still the same—you're wasting your time loving me, Ethan. If, indeed, you do,' she added dismissively.

'Oh, I do. And it's my time to waste,' he murmured close behind her, the warmth of his breath warming the nape of her neck.

Her hands clenched into fists at her sides as she forced herself not to flinch at his closeness. 'I would like you to leave now.'

'No.'

She did turn to face him then, frowning incredulously. 'I want you to leave,' she repeated tensely.

Ethan stayed where he was. 'And I said no. The rattle you showed Andrea this morning—it was Jonathan's, wasn't it?' he probed gently.

'Ethan—'

'Wasn't it?' he persisted forcefully.

'Well…yes. But—'

'The first of any of his things you've ever given away?' Ethan continued his probing.

She swayed slightly, closing her eyes, instantly seeing those two big brown boxes in her second bedroom that contained everything that had ever been Jonathan's; she had never been able to bear parting with any of it.

'Olivia!' Ethan was breathing shakily as he once again took her into his arms. 'I can't even begin to imagine what losing the two of them did to you.' He spoke into her hair. 'Nor can I blame you for wanting to shut yourself away emotionally these last ten years— if only so that you could never be hurt in that way again. But don't you see, my darling, that it's too late to think you can carry on doing that any longer? By giving Andrea that toy this morning, perhaps without realising what you were doing, you began the painful process of letting go—'

'Rubbish!' Olivia denied heatedly, trying to escape Ethan's arms—but failing as he simply tightened his hold on her. 'It was only a teething ring, for goodness' sake!' She glared up at him.

'It was Jonathan's teething ring,' he insisted evenly.

Olivia's anger towards him deepened. 'Well, he's hardly going to need it again, is he—? I can't believe I just said that!' she groaned emotionally, burying her face in her hands. 'He was so beautiful, Ethan. So young, and sweet—such a happy baby.' She shook her head. 'And ultimately so utterly vulnerable…!' She began to cry then, deep heart-rending sobs, the tears falling like hot rain down her cheeks.

Ethan's arms tightened about her as he lifted her up and carried her over to one of the armchairs, sitting down with her cradled in his arms, her head resting on his shoulder as he let her continue to cry.

How long they sat like that Olivia had no idea, only knew that finally she felt exhausted by her own grief. And so very aware of Ethan's closeness…

She shook her head. 'I can't love you, Ethan,' she told him gruffly.

'As I said—can't or won't…?' he returned softly.

She raised her head to look at him. 'Does it matter which?'

'Of course it matters,' he said.

Olivia gave a scathing snort. 'Don't you already have enough women in your harem without trying to add me to their number?'

Ethan remained unmoved by her deliberate attempt to alienate him. 'I'm a fashion photographer, Olivia. Sometimes I work from home.' He shrugged. 'There is no woman in my life. Only you. Each and every one of those women you've seen coming to my apartment has been there for one reason only—so that I can photograph them. Remind me to show you my studio in the second bedroom when we go back upstairs,' he said, as she continued to look sceptical.

He was *that* Sherbourne...! Why had she never thought of such a simple explanation for the comings and goings to Ethan's apartment of those numerous women? Because it had been easier to think of Ethan as a rake and a womaniser, and not a world-famous fashion-photographer, came the instant answer to that question!

'I'm not going back upstairs with you—'

'Oh, yes, you are,' he assured her. 'Can't you see, Olivia? It's too late. For both of us. I wasn't exactly looking for love myself, you know,' he added teasingly. 'I've spent the last twenty years perfecting the art of the brief, meaningless relationship,' he said. 'But you, with your huge expressive eyes, that ethereal beauty, the snappy dialogue you've developed to hide your own vulnerability—you've crept under my defences, Olivia. And, although I may not have been looking for love, I do not intend turning my back on the gift now that it's been given to me.'

A gift... Yes, love was a gift. Could she really take the risk of loving someone again, of perhaps losing them?

But, as Ethan had said, did she really have a choice, when she was already in love with him? Was denying him now, ejecting him from her life, going to make any difference to the way she felt about him?

She wasn't seriously thinking of accepting his proposal, was she...?

To spend every day and night with Ethan… To wake up beside him in the morning and know that he loved her as much as she loved him… To come home to him each evening and know that he had simply been counting the hours, as she had, until they could be together again… To have dinner with him every night… To lie in his arms every night… To do all the simple day-to-day things together, like shopping, and preparing food…

All the things she had once done with Simon…

'Would Simon have wanted you to spend the rest of your life alone?' Ethan's arms tightened about her as he seemed to sense the drift of her thoughts. 'Would you have wanted that for him if he had been the one left behind?'

'Of course not,' she gasped, her face paling as she realised what she had just said. 'I loved Simon very much,' she told Ethan defensively—but realised even as she did so that she had used the past tense…

'Of course you did,' Ethan agreed. 'And loving me doesn't mean you have to stop loving him,' he assured her firmly. 'I'm going to ask you again, Olivia.' He straightened in the chair, looking her fully in the face now, his gaze intense. 'Will you marry me? Will you let me love you? Will you love me in return? Will you marry me so that we can spend the rest of our lives together?'

Olivia swallowed hard, her heart leaping at the words, her cheeks flushed, her pulse beating erratically in her chest.

Could she do that? Could she make what was, after all, a leap of faith?

* * *

'Will she?' Faith groaned, chewing worriedly on her bottom lip as she watched Olivia and Ethan together.

'Shh,' Mrs Heavenly admonished impatiently. 'Or we'll miss her answer!'

EPILOGUE

'OLIVIA...? Darling, I'm home!' Ethan called out. 'I've got the tree.' He barely paused as he put his car keys down on the tray in the hallway. 'But I'll need some help bringing it into the— Oomph!' He groaned breathlessly as Olivia ran from the kitchen to launch herself into his arms. 'Hello, my darling.' He grinned down at her before kissing her soundly on the lips. 'Mmm, you smell good.' He buried his face in her shoulder-length hair.

'I've been preparing and steaming the Christmas pudding this afternoon.' Olivia laughed happily. 'With a little help from my friends, of course,' she added indulgently, barely having time to move out of the way as two small tornadoes came hurtling down the hallway.

'Daddy!' the duo cried together, even as they launched themselves into their father's waiting arms.

Olivia's smile widened as she watched their small daughters snuggle up to Ethan, one in each arm, the two of them giggling happily as their father tickled them by blowing lightly on their chubby necks.

At two years old, Emily and Daisy were as alike as two peas in a pod—dark-haired, brown-eyed little charmers. Much like their father, Olivia thought indulgently as she gazed lovingly at her husband.

'Did you make a big Christmas pudding?' he was teasing his daughters now. 'We have Nanny and Grandad coming to spend Christmas with us this year.' He smiled at Olivia with this mention of her parents. 'And Andrew, Shelley and Andrea.'

Olivia never ceased to wonder at the transformation there had been to her life these last three years: her reconciliation with her parents, her marriage to Ethan, their move to this large house in the country, Andrew's marriage to Shelley, the birth of the twins a year after their own wedding...

Although it was her love and marriage that she cherished the most. Ethan was a wonderful husband—caring, considerate, loving her so completely she could never doubt their future together.

It truly was a marriage made in heaven...

Mrs Heavenly, smiling from above, with tears of happiness in her eyes, could only nod silently.

There are 24 timeless classics in the Mills & Boon® 100th Birthday Collection

Two of these beautiful stories are out each month. Make sure you collect them all!

If you have missed any of these books, log on to www.millsandboon.co.uk to order your copies online.